# THE
# STAINLESS STEEL RAT
# SINGS THE BLUES

# THE STAINLESS STEEL RAT SINGS THE BLUES

## HARRY HARRISON

BANTAM BOOKS
*New York  Toronto  London  Sydney  Auckland*

THE STAINLESS STEEL RAT SINGS THE BLUES

A Bantam Spectra Book / April 1994

SPECTRA and the portrayal of a boxed "s" are trademarks of Bantam Books, a division of Bantam Doubleday Dell Publishing Group, Inc.

Library of Congress Cataloging-in-Publication Data

Harrison, Harry.
The stainless steel rat sings the blues / by Harry Harrison.
p. cm.
ISBN 0-553-09612-5 : $19.95
1. DiGriz, James Bolivar (Fictitious character)—Fiction.
I. Title.
PS3558.A667S72   1994
813'.54—dc20            93-31809
CIP

*Published simultaneously in the United States and Canada*

Bantam Books are published by Bantam Books, a division of Bantam Doubleday Dell Publishing Group, Inc. Its trademark, consisting of the words "Bantam Books" and the portrayal of a rooster, is Registered in U.S. Patent and Trademark Office and in other countries. Marca Registrada. Bantam Books, 1540 Broadway, New York, New York 10036.

PRINTED IN THE UNITED STATES OF AMERICA

RRH   0 9 8 7 6 5 4 3 2 1

# THE
# STAINLESS STEEL RAT
# SINGS THE BLUES

# CHAPTER 1

Walking up the wall had not been easy. But walking across the ceiling was turning out to be completely impossible. Until I realized that I was going about it the wrong way. It seemed obvious when I thought about it. When I held onto the ceiling with my hands I could not move my feet. So I switched off the molebind gloves and swung down, hanging only from the soles of my boots. The blood rushed to my head—as well it might—bringing with it a surge of nausea and a sensation of great unease.

What was I doing here, hanging upside down from the ceiling of the Mint, watching the machine below stamp out five-hundred-thousand-credit coins? They jingled and fell into the waiting baskets—so the answer to that question was pretty obvious. I nearly fell after them as I cut the power on one foot. I swung it forward in a giant step and slammed it solidly against the ceiling again as I turned the binding energy back on. A generator in the boot emitted a field of the same binding energy that holds molecules together, making my foot, at least temporarily, a part of the ceiling. As long as the power was on.

A few more long steps and I was over the baskets. I fumbled at my waist, trying to ignore the dizziness, and pulled out the cord from my oversized belt buckle. Bending double until I could reach up to the ceiling, I pushed the knob at the end against the plaster and switched it on. The molebind field clamped hard and I released my feet. To hang, swinging, right side up now, while the blood seeped out of my florid face.

"Come on Jim—no hanging about," I advised myself. "The alarm will go off any second now."

Right on cue the sirens screamed, the lights blinked, while a gargantuan hooter thundered through the walls. I did not tell myself that I told me so. No time. Thumb on the power button so that the immensely strong, almost invisible, single-molecule cord whirred out of the buckle and dropped me swiftly down. When my outstretched hands clinked among the coins I stopped. Opened my attaché case and dragged it clanking through the coins until it was full of the shining, shimmering beauties.

Closed and sealed it as the tiny motor buzzed and dragged me up to the ceiling again. My feet struck and stuck: I switched off power to the lifting lug.

And the door opened below me.

"Somebody coulda come in here!" the guard shouted, his weapon nosing about him. "The door alarm went off."

"Maybe—but I don't see nothin'," the second guard said.

They looked down and around. But never up. I hoped. Feeling the sweat rolling up my face. Collecting there. Dropping.

I watched with horror as the droplets spattered down onto the guard's helmet.

"Next room!" he shouted, his voice drowning out the splat of perspiration. They rushed out, the door closed, I walked across the ceiling, crawled down the wall, slumped with exhaustion on the floor.

"Ten seconds, no more," I admonished. Survival was a harsh taskmaster. What had seemed like a good idea at the time maybe really was a good idea. But right now I was very sorry I had ever seen the newsflash.

*Ceremonial opening of new Mint on Paskönjak . . . planet often called Mintworld . . . first half-million-credit coins ever issued . . . dignitaries and press invited.*

It had been like the sound of the starting gun to a sprinter.

I was off. A week later I was stepping out of the space terminal on Paskönjak, bag in hand and forged press credentials in pocket. Even the massed troops and tough security had not tempered my madness. The machines in my case were immune from detection by any known security apparatus; the case projected a totally false image of its contents when radiation hit it. My step had been light, my smile broad.

Now my face was ashen and my legs trembled with fatigue as I pushed myself to my feet.

"Look calm, look collected—think innocence."

I swallowed a calm-and-collected pill that was coated with instant uppers. One, two, three paces to the door, my face flushed with pride, my gait noble, my conscience pure.

I put on my funky bejeweled spectacles and looked through the door. The ultrasound image was fuzzy. But clear enough to reveal figures hurrying past. When they were gone I unlocked the door, slipped through and let it close behind me.

Saw the rest of my party of journalists being pushed down the corridor by screaming, gun-waving troops. Turned and marched firmly away in the opposite direction and around the bend.

The guard stationed there lowered his gun and pointed it at my belt buckle.

"*La necesejo estas ĉi tie?*" I said, smiling smarmily.

"What you say? What you doin' here?"

"Indeed?" I snorted through widened nostrils. "Rather short on education, particularly a knowledge of Esperanto, aren't we? If you must know, speaking in the vulgar argot of this planet—I was told that the men's room was down here."

"Well it ain't. Da udder way."

"You're too kind."

I turned and strolled diffidently down the hall. Had taken three steps before reality penetrated his sluggish synapses.

"Come back here, you!"

I stopped and turned about, pointed past him. "Down that way?" I asked. The gas projector I had palmed when my back was turned towards him hissed briefly. His eyes closed and he dropped; I took the gun from his limp hands as he fell by. Placed it on his sleeping chest since it was of no help to me. Walked briskly past him and pushed open the door to the emergency stairs. Closed and leaned against it and breathed very deeply. Then took out the map that had been in the press kit and poked my finger on the symbol for stairs. Now, down to the storeroom . . . footsteps sounded below.

Up. Quietly on soft soles. A change of plan was very much in order since the alarm had sounded, ruling out a simple exit with the crowd. Up, five, six flights until the steps ended in a door labeled KROV. Which probably meant roof in the local language.

There were three different alarms that I disabled before I pushed the door open and slipped through. Looked around at the usual rooftop clutter; water tanks, vents, aircon units—and a good-sized smokestack puffing out pollution. Perfect.

The moneybag clunked as I dropped all my incriminating weapons and tools into it. My belt buckle twisted open and I took out the reel and motor. Attached the molebind plug from the suspension cord to the bag, then lowered it all down the chimney. Reaching down as far as I could I secured the reel mechanism to the inside of the pipe.

Done. It would wait there as long as needed, until all the excitement calmed down. An investment waiting to be collected you might say. Then, armed only with my innocence, I retraced my course back down the stairs and on to the ground floor.

The door opened and closed silently and there was a guard, back turned, standing close enough to touch. Which I did, tapping him on the shoulder. He shrieked, jumped aside, turned, lifted his gun.

"Didn't mean to startle you," I said sweetly. "Afraid I got separated from my party. The press group . . ."

"Sergeant, I got someone," he burbled into the microphone on his shoulder. "Me, yeah, Private Izmet, post eleven. Right. Hold him. Got that." He pointed the gun between my eyes. "Don't move!"

"I have no intention of that, I assure you."

I admired my fingernails, plucked a bit of fluff from my jacket, whistled; tried to ignore the wavering gun muzzle. There was the thud of running feet and a squad led by a grim-looking sergeant rushed up.

"Good afternoon, Sergeant. Can you tell me why this soldier is pointing his weapon at me? Or rather why you are all pointing your weapons at me?"

"Grab his case. Cuff him. Bring him." A man of few words, the sergeant.

The elevator they hustled me to had not been marked on the map issued to the journalists. Nor had the map even hinted at the many levels below the ground floor that penetrated deep into the bowels of the earth. The pressure hit my eardrums as we dropped—about as many floors down as you usually go up in a skyscraper. My stomach sank as well as I realized I had bitten off a good deal more than I could possibly chew. Pushed out at some subterranean level, dragged through locked, barred gates, one after another, until we finally reached a singularly depressing room. Traditionally bare with unshielded lights and a backless stool. I sighed and sat.

My attempts at conversation were ignored, as was my press pass. Which was taken from me along with my shoes—then the rest of my clothes. I pulled on the robe of itchy black burlap that they gave me, dropped back into the chair and made no attempt to outstare my guards.

To be frank this was a kind of a low point, made even lower when the effects of the calm-and-collected pill began to wear off. Just about the time my morale hit bottom the loud-speaker gurgled incomprehensible instructions and I was hur-ried down the hall to another room. The lights and stool were the same—but this time they faced a steel desk with an even steelier-eyed officer behind it. His glare spoke for him as he pointed to my dissected clothing, bag, shoes.

"I am Colonel Neuredan—and you are in trouble."

"Do you always treat interstellar journalists like this?"

"Your identity is false." His voice had all the warmth of two rocks being grated together. "Your shoes contain molebind projectors . . ."

"There's no law against that!"

"There is on Paskönjak. There is a law against anything that threatens the security of the Mint and the Interstellar Credits produced here."

"I've done nothing wrong."

"*Everything* that you have done has been wrong. Attempt-ing to deceive our security with false identification, stunning a guard, penetrating the Mint without supervision—these are all crimes under our law. What you have committed so far makes you liable for fourteen concurrent life sentences." His grim voice grew even grimmer. "But there is even worse than that—"

"What could be worse than fourteen life sentences?" De-spite my efforts at calm control I could hear my voice cracking.

"Death. That is the penalty for stealing from the Mint."

"I haven't stolen anything!" Definitely a quaver now.

"That will be determined very shortly. When the decision was made to mint five-hundred-thousand-credit coins every precaution was taken to prevent their theft. Integral to their fabric is a transponder that listens for a specific signal at a specific frequency. It answers and reveals the location of the coin."

"Stupid," I said with more bravado than I felt. "Won't work here. Not with all the coins you have made—"

"All now safe behind ten feet of solid lead. Radiation-proof. If there are any other coins not in our custody the signal will sound."

Right on cue I heard the pealing of bells in the distance. The iron face of my inquisitor was touched by a fleeting cold smile.

"The signal," he said. We sat in silence for long seconds. Until the door burst open and the hurrying guards dropped a very familiar bag onto the desk. He lifted the end slowly and the coins jangled forth.

"So that's what they look like. I never . . ."

"Silence!" he thundered. "These were removed from the minting room. They were found suspended in the chimney from the smelter. Along with these other objects."

"Proves nothing."

"Proves *everything!*" Quick as a snake he grabbed my hands, slammed them onto a plate on his desk. A hologram of my fingerprints appeared instantly on the air above.

"Any prints lifted from the coins?" he asked over his shoulder.

"Many," a spectral voice responded. A portion of the desk top rose up bearing what appeared to be photographic prints. He looked at them and for the second time I was treated to the sight of that frigid smile as he dropped the prints through a slot. A second hologram floated in the air beside the first, moved over and merged with it as he touched the controls.

The double image flickered and became one.

"Identical!" he said triumphantly. "You can tell me your name if you wish. So it can be spelled correctly on your tombstone. But only if you wish."

"What do you mean tombstone? And what do you mean death sentence? That's illegal by galactic law!"

"There is no galactic law down here," he intoned with a voice like a funeral march. "There is only the law of the Mint. Judgment is final."

"The trial . . ." I said feebly, visions of lawyers, appeals, torts and documents dancing in my head.

There was no mercy in his voice now, no touch of the tiniest of iceberg smiles on his lips.

"The penalty for theft in the Mint is death. The trial takes place *after* the execution."

# CHAPTER 2

I am still young—and it did not look like I was going to get any older. My dedication to a life of crime had led to a far shorter lifespan than could normally be expected. Here I was, not yet twenty years old. A veteran who had fought in two wars, had been imprisoned and drafted, who had been depressed by the death of my good friend The Bishop, been impressed by Mark Forer the great Artificial Intelligence. Was that it? Had I had it? No more to life than that? All over.

"Never!" I shouted aloud, but the two guards merely gripped my arms the harder and pushed me along the corridor. A third armed guard went ahead and unlocked the cell door, while the one behind me prodded my kidneys with the barrel of his gun.

They were good and they took no chances. They were big and mean and I was small and lean. Shivering with fear, I was crouching even lower. Once the cell door was open the guard with the keys turned towards me and unlocked my handcuffs.

Then gasped as my knee caught him in the stomach and knocked him back into the cell. At the same time I grabbed the two guards beside me by the wrists, crossed my arms with a single spasmodic burst of effort that pulled the two of them crashing together; their skulls bonked nicely. At the same instant I lashed backward—catching the fourth guard on the bridge of his nose with the back of my head. Everything happening at approximately the same time.

Two seconds ago I had been bound and captive.

Now one guard was out of sight, groaning in the cell. Two more holding their heads and howling, the fourth one clutching a bloody nose. They hadn't been expecting this: I had.

I ran. Back the way we had come and through the still-open door. Hoarse, angry cries were cut off as I slammed it shut, locked it. The thick panel shook as heavy bodies thudded against the other side.

"Got you!" a victorious voice shouted and rough hands grabbed me. He could not know by touch that I was a Black Belt? He found out the hard way.

Eyes closed, breathing easily, he just lay there and made no protest as I stripped him of uniform and weapons. Nor did he thank me when I draped my burlap robe over his pale form, hiding his black lace undies from prying eyes. His clothes were not too bad a fit. Not too good either with the cap tilting forward over my eyes. But it would have to do.

There were three doors leading from this room. The one that I had locked was pounding and bouncing in its frame: next to it was the one that we had come in through. It didn't take much intelligence to use the unconscious guard's keys to open the third one.

It led to a storage room. Dark shelves, filled with nameless objects, vanished away into the distance. Not too promising— but I was in no position to choose. I executed a quick leap back to the entrance door, unlocked it and threw it open, then dived ahead into the storage room. As I closed this final door behind me, even before I could lock it, there was a mighty crash and screams of anger as the assaultees finally broke the door down.

Misdirection wouldn't last long. Run past the shelves. Hide here? No—there would be a thorough search. A door at the far end, bolted on the inside. I opened it a crack and looked at the empty room beyond. Opened and stepped through.

And stopped quite still as the guards who were flattened against the wall all pointed guns at me.

"Shoot him!" Colonel Neuredan ordered.

"I'm unarmed!" My gun slid across the floor as I threw my hands into the air. Fingers quivered on triggers—it was all over.

"Don't shoot—I want him alive. For the moment."

I stood frozen, not breathing until the trigger fingers relaxed. Looked up and quickly found the security bug in the ceiling. Must be one in every room and corridor down here. They had been watching me all the time. A good try, Jim. The Colonel grated his teeth horribly and stabbed a finger in my direction.

"Take him. Chain him. Bind him. Bring him."

This was all done with ruthless efficiency. My toes dragged along the floor as I was whisked back to the cell, stripped at gunpoint, thrown to the floor with my black robe thrown on top of me. The door clanged shut and I was alone. Very much alone.

"Cheer up, Jim, you've been in worse trouble before," I chirped smilingly. Then snarled, "When?"

Back in the pits again. My abortive attempt at escape had only gained me a few bruises.

"This can't be it!" I shouted. "It can't all end just like this."

"It can—and it will," the Colonel's funereal voice intoned as the cell door opened again. A dozen guns were pointed at me as a guard brought in a tray with a bottle of champagne on it and a single glass.

I watched in stupefied disbelief as he twisted the cork out. There was a pop and a gush as the golden fluid filled the glass. He handed it to me.

"What's this, what's this?" I mumbled, staring wide-eyed at the rising bubbles.

"Your last request," Neuredan said. "That and a cigarette."

He took one from a package and lit it, holding it out to

me. I shook my head. "I don't smoke." He ground the cigarette under his heel. "Anyway—champagne and a cigarette—
that's not *my* last request."

"Yes it is. Forms of last request are standardized by law.
Drink."

I drank. It tasted all right. I belched and handed back the
glass. "I'll take a refill." Anything to gain time, to think. I
watched the wine being poured and my brain was dull and
empty. "You never told me about the . . . execution."

"Do you want to know?"

"Not really."

"Then I will be pleased to tell you. I assure you that there
was extensive deliberation over the correct method to be used.
Thought was given to the firing squad, electrocution, poison
gas—a number of possibilities were actively considered when
the law was passed. But all of them involve someone pulling a
switch or a trigger, and that would not be humane to the
someone."

"Humane! What about the prisoner?"

"Of no importance. Your death has been decreed and will
take place as soon as possible. This is what will happen. You
will be taken to a sealed chamber and chained there. The entrance will be locked. After this the chamber will be flooded
with water by an automatic device actuated by your body heat.
It is always there, always turned on. You alone will be respon-
sible for your own execution. Now isn't that quite quite humane?"

"Drowning is humane all of a sudden?"

"Possibly not. But you will be left a pistol containing a
single bullet. You can commit suicide if you wish to."

I opened my mouth to tell him what I thought of their
humanity, but I was seized by many hands and dragged forward before I could speak. The glass was whisked away—and
so was I. Deep down to a dank chamber, walls damp with
water and covered with moss. A cuff was clamped around my

ankle; a chain ran from it to a staple in the wall. They all exited except for the Colonel who stood with his hand on the operating lever of the thick, undoubtedly watertight, door.

He grinned in victorious triumph, bent over and placed an antique pistol on the floor. As I dived for it the door shut and sealed with a final thud.

Was this really the end? I turned the pistol over in my hands, saw the dull shape of the single cartridge. End of Jim diGriz, end of the Stainless Steel Rat, end of everything.

There was the distant thunk of a valve opening and cold water gushed down on me from a thick pipe in the ceiling. It gurgled and slopped, covering my feet, then quickly up to my ankles. When it reached my waist I lifted the gun and looked at it. Not much of a choice. The water rose steadily. Covered my chest, up to my chin. I shuddered.

Then the water stopped splashing down. It was cold and I was shivering uncontrollably. The light in the waterproof fixture revealed only stone wall, dark water.

"What are you playing at *bastardaĉoj*?" I shouted. "Humane torture to go with your humane murder?"

A moment later I got my answer. The level began to drop.

"I was right—torturers!" I bellowed. "Torture first—then murder. And you call yourself civilized. Why are you doing this?"

The last of the water gurgled down the drain and the door slowly opened. I aimed the pistol at it. I wouldn't mind drowning if I could take the cretinous colonel or the sadistic sergeant with me.

Something dark appeared through the partly open door. The gun banged and the bullet thudded into it. A briefcase.

"Cease fire!" a male voice called out. "I am your lawyer."

"He only has one bullet, you're safe," I heard the Colonel say.

The briefcase came hesitantly into the room, carried by a gray-haired man who was wearing the traditional gold-flecked and diamond decorated black suit that adorned lawyers throughout the galaxy.

"I am your court-appointed lawyer, Pederasis Narcoses."

"What good will you do me—if the trial will be after my execution?"

"None. But that is the law. I will have to interview you now to enable me to conduct your defense at the trial."

"This is madness—I'll be dead!"

"That is correct. But it is the law." He turned to the Colonel. "I must be alone with my client. That is also the law."

"You have ten minutes, no longer."

"That will suffice. Admit my assistant in five minutes. He has the court papers and the will."

The door thunked shut and Narcoses opened his briefcase and took out a plastic bottle filled with a greenish liquid. He removed the top and handed it to me.

"Drink this, all of it. I'll hold the gun."

I handed him the weapon, took the bottle, smelled it and coughed. "Horrible. Why should I drink it?"

"Because I told you to. It is of vital importance and you have no choice."

Which was true—and what difference would it make anyway? I glugged it down. The champagne had tasted a lot better.

"I will now explain," he said, recapping the bottle and putting it back into his briefcase. "You have just drunk a thirty-day poison. This is a computer-generated complex of toxins that are neutral now—but which will kill you horribly in exactly thirty days if you are not given the antidote. Which is also computer-generated and impossible to duplicate."

He jumped back quite smartly when I leaped at him. But the chain on my ankle would not quite reach. My fingers snapped ineffectually just in front of his throat.

"If you will cease clawing at the air I will explain," Narcoses said with an air of weary sophistication. Had he done this kind of thing before I wondered? I folded my arms and stepped back.

"Much better. Although I am a lawyer licensed to practice on this planet, I am also a representative of the Galactic League."

"Wonderful. The Paskönjakians want to drown me—you poison me. I thought this was a galaxy of peace?"

"You are wasting time. I am here to free you, under certain conditions. The League has need of a criminal. One who is both skilled and reliable. Which is an oxymoron. You have proved your criminalistic ability by your almost-successful theft. The poison guarantees your reliability. Do I assume that you will cooperate? At the minimum you have a life extension of thirty days."

"Yes, sure, you're on. Not that I have a choice."

"You don't." He looked at the watch set into his little fingernail and stepped aside as the door opened. A chubby, bearded youth came in with a sheaf of papers.

"Excellent," Narcoses said. "You have the will?" The young man nodded. The door was closed and sealed again.

"Five minutes," Narcoses said.

The newcomer pulled down a zipper that sealed his one-piece suit. Took off the suit—and a lot of flesh with it. The suit was padded. He was not fat at all, but lean and muscular quite like me. When he peeled off the fake beard I realized that he looked exactly like me. I blinked rapidly as I stared at my own face.

"Only four minutes left diGriz. Put on the suit. I'll fix the beard."

The well-built and handsome stranger pulled on my discarded robe. Stepped aside when Narcoses took a key from his pocket, bent and unlocked the restraining cuff on my ankle. Handed it to the other who emotionlessly bent and snapped it to his own ankle.

"Why—why are you doing this?" I asked him.

He said nothing, just leaned over to retrieve the gun.

"I'll need another bullet," he said. With my voice.

"The Colonel will supply it," Narcoses said. Then I remembered something else he had said just moments ago.

"You called me diGriz. You know my name!"

"I know a lot more than that," he said pressing the beard and mustache into position on my face. "Carry these papers. Follow me out of here. Keep your mouth shut."

All of which I was very happy to do. With one last look at my imprisoned self I trotted forth to freedom.

# CHAPTER 3

I trotted behind Narcoses, clutching the papers and trying to think bearded and fat. The guards were ignoring us, watching instead with sadistic fascination as one of their number started to close the watertight door.

"Wait," the Colonel said, opening a small box and taking out a cartridge. He looked up as I passed, stared me straight in the face. I felt perspiration bursting from my pores. The momentary glance must have lasted about a subjective hour. Then he kept on turning and called out to the guard.

"Open that again you idiot! I load the gun *then* you close the door. When that has been done this business will be over with once and for all."

We turned a corner and the noxious group vanished from sight behind us. Silently, as ordered, I followed the lawyer through many a guarded portal, into an elevator, out of it and then through one final door, escaping the Mint at last. Letting out a great sigh of relief as we went past the armed guards and headed for the waiting ground car.

"I—"

"Silence! Into the car. Speak to me in the office about a salary raise—not before."

Narcoses must know things that I didn't. Detector bugs in the ornamental trees we were passing? Acoustic microphones aimed our way? I realized now that my carefully planned crime had apparently been a disaster from the moment I had conceived it.

The driver was silent as a tomb—and about as attractive. I watched the buildings stream by, then the outskirts of the city appeared. We drove on until we reached a small building in a leafy suburb. The front door opened as we approached, then closed behind us apparently without human intervention. The same thing happened to the inner door which was tastefully labeled with jewel-studded gold letters PEDERASIS NARCOSES—*Attorney at Laws*. It closed silently and I wheeled about and pointed a menacing finger at him.

"You knew about me even before I landed on this planet."

"Of course. As soon as your false credentials were filed the investigation began."

"So you stood by and let me plot and plan and commit a crime and get sentenced to death—without making any attempt to interfere?"

"That's right."

"That's criminal! More of a crime than my crime."

"Not really. You were always going to be plucked out of that terminal swimming pool in any case. We just wanted to see how well you did."

"How did I do?"

"Very good—for a lad your age. You got the job."

"Well good for me. But what about my double—the bloke who took my place?"

"That bloke, as you refer to him, is one of the finest and most expensive humanoid robots that money can afford. Which money will not be wasted since the doctor who is now performing the postmortem is in our pay. The incident is closed."

"Wonderful," I sighed, dropping limply onto the couch. "Look, can I get a drink? It has been a long day. No spirits however—a beer will do fine."

"A capital idea. I will join you."

A tiny but well-stocked bar unfolded from one wall; the dispenser produced two chilled brews. I gulped and smacked.

"Excellent. If I have only thirty days to go shouldn't you be telling me about what you want me to do?"

"In good time," he said, sitting down across from me. "Captain Varod asked me to send his regards. And to convey the message that he knew you were lying when you promised to give up a life of crime."

"So he had me watched?"

"You're catching on. After this last criminal assignment for us you will become an honest man. Or else."

"Who are you to talk!" I sneered and drained the glass. "A crooked shyster who is theoretically paid to uphold the law. Yet you stand by and let the thugs here on Paskönjak pass legislation to have trials *after* an execution—then you employ a criminal to commit a criminal act. Not what I would call sincerely law-abiding."

"First," he said, lifting a finger in a very legalistic way, "we have never condoned the secret law in the Mint. It was only recently produced by the overly-paranoid management here. Yours was the first arrest—and will be the last. There have been numerous job replacements already. Secondly," another finger rose to join the first, "the League has never condoned violence or criminal acts. This is the first occurrence and has been produced by an unusual series of circumstances. After great deliberation the decision was made to do it just this one time. And never again."

"Millions might believe that," I sneered disbelievingly. "Isn't it time you told me what the job is?"

"No—because I don't know myself. My vote was cast against this entire operation so I have been included out. Professor Van Diver will brief you."

"But what about the thirty-day poison?"

"You will be contacted on the twenty-ninth day." He stood up and went to the door. "It is against my principles to wish you good luck."

This was his puritanical pontificatory exit line. Because as he went out an elderly type with a white beard and a monocle entered.

"Professor Van Diver I presume?"

"Indeed," he said extending a damp, limp hand for me to shake. "You must be the volunteer with the *nom de guerre* of Jim about whose presence I was informed, who would await me here. It was very good of you to undertake what can only be called a rather diligent and difficult assignment."

"Rather," I intoned, falling into his academic mode of speech. "Is there any remote possibility that I might be informed of the nature of this assignment?"

"Of course. I have the requisite authority to provide augmentive information to you concerning the history and tragic circumstance of the loss. Another individual, who shall be nameless, will supply the assistance that you will require. I shall begin with the circumstances that occurred a little over twenty years ago . . ."

"A beer. I must have refreshment. Will you join me?"

"I abstain from all alcoholic and caffeine-containing beverages." He glared at me glassily through his menacing monocle as I refilled my mug. I sipped and sat and waved him into action. His voice washed over me in turgid waves and soon had me half-asleep—but the content of his talk woke me up fast enough. He went on far too long, with far too many digressions, but despite this it was fascinating stuff to listen to.

A stripped-down version wouldn't have been half as much fun for him and would have taken only a few minutes to tell. Simply, Galaksia Universitato had sent an expedition to a reported archeological site on a distant world—where they had uncovered an artifact of non-human origin.

"You must be kidding," I said. "Mankind has explored a great part of the galaxy in the last thirty-two thousand years and no trace of an alien race has ever been found."

He sniffed loudly. "I do not 'kid' as you say in your simple demotic. I have pictorial proof here, photographs sent back by the expedition. The artifact was uncovered in a stratum at least a million years old and resembles nothing in any data base existent in the known universe."

He took a print from his inner pocket and passed it over to me. I took it and looked at it, then turned it around since there was no indication of which was top or bottom. A twisted hunk of incongruous angles and forms resembling nothing I had ever seen before.

"It looks alien enough to be alien," I said. Looking at it was beginning to hurt my eyes so I dropped it onto the table. "What does it do, or what is it made of or whatever?"

"I haven't the slightest idea since it was never conveyed to the university. It was, I must say, interrupted in its journey and it is essential that it be recovered."

"Pretty sloppy way to handle the only alien artifact in the universe."

"That is beyond the scope of my authority and not for me to say. But I am authorized to unperfunctorily predicate that it must be found and returned. At any cost—which sums I am duly authorized to pay. Officers of the Galactic League have assured me that you, pseudonymous Jim, have volunteered to find and return the artifact. They have convinced me that you, as young as you are, are a specialist in these matters. I can only wish you best of luck—and look forward to meeting you again when you return with that which we desire the most."

He exited then and a bald, uniformed naval officer entered in his place. Closed the door and glared at me with a steely gaze. I glared back.

"Are you the one who is finally going to tell me what is going on?" I asked.

"Damn right," he growled. "Damn fool idea—but the only one we have going. I am Admiral Benbow, head of League Navy Security. Those dumbhead academics let the most price-

less object in the universe slip through their fingers—now we
have to pick up the pieces and run with the ball."

The Admiral's mixed metaphors were as bad as the professor's academese. Was clear speaking becoming a lost art?

"Come on," I said. "Simply tell me what happened and
what I am supposed to do."

"Right." He slammed down into a chair. "If that is a beer
I'll have one too. No I won't. A double, no a treble high-
octane whisky. No ice. Do it."

The robobar supplied our drinks. He drained his while I
was just lifting mine.

"Now hear this. The expedition concerned was returning
from their planetary dig when their ship experienced communication difficulties. Worried about navigation they landed on
the nearest planet, which unhappily and tragically turned out
to be Liokukae."

"Why unhappily and tragically?"

"Shut up and listen. We got them and their ship back relatively intact. But without the artifact. For certain reasons we
could do no more. That is why your services have been en-
gaged."

"So now you are going to tell me about those certain reasons."

He coughed and looked away, stood and refilled his glass
before speaking again. If I didn't know better I would have
said that the seasoned old space dog was embarrassed.

"You have to understand that keeping the galactic peace is
our role and our goal. This is not always possible. There are
sometimes individuals, even groups, that are impervious to our
attentions. Violent people, some apparently incurably insane,
obnoxious. Despite everything that we can do they remain immune to our blandishments, impervious to our help." He
gulped down the dregs and I had the feeling that we were
finally getting to the truth.

"Since we cannot kill them we—and you realize only the

highest authorities know what I am about to tell you—we so to speak arrange, see to it that they are, well, transported to Liokukae to live the sort of life they prefer to live. Without endangering the peaceful cultures of the union—"

"A galactic garbage dump!" I cried aloud. "Where you holier-than-thou bigots sweep your failures under the carpet! No wonder you keep this a top-secret secret."

"Just knock off the superior attitude cagal, diGriz. I know your record—and in my book it stinks. But we have you by the short and curlies since you drank the seven-hundred-and-twenty-hour poison, so you will do just as I say. So now I'm going to fill you in with all the loathsome details re Liokukae, let you see what information we have. Then you will come up with a plan for getting that thing back. You have no choice."

"Thanks. What resources do I have?"

"Limitless resources, unrestricted funds, boundless support. Every planet in the galaxy contributes to Galaksia Universitato. They have so many credits that they make the super-rich look super-poor. I want you to take them to the cleaners."

"Now you are talking my language! For the first time I have some interest in this poisonous project. Bring on the records—and some food—and I will see what I can do."

Not very much I thought to myself after hours of reading and rereading the thin file, while eating a number of stale and tasteless sandwiches. The Admiral was slumped asleep in the armchair and snoring like a rocket exhaust. There were no answers here, so some questions were very much in order. Which gave me the sweet pleasure of waking him up. A few good shakes did it and those nasty little red eyes glared into mine.

"You better have a good reason for that."

"I do. How much do you personally know about Liokukae?"

"Everything, you dimwit. That is why I am here."

"It seems to be pretty tightly sealed up."

"Pretty tightly is not the way I would describe it. Hermetically sealed, guarded, patrolled, watched, locked tight, quarantined—take your pick. Food and medicines are shipped in. Nothing comes out."

"Do they have their own doctors?"

"No. Medical teams are stationed there in the hospital inside the landing station—which is built like a fortress. And before you even ask—the answer is no. What little trust there is between the Navy and the Liokukaers involves the medical services. They come to us and we treat them. Let them suspect for an instant that the medicos are involved in hanky-panky and the trust is gone. Disease and death would be certain. We're not taking a chance on that."

"If the rest of the civilized galaxy doesn't know about them—what do they know about us?"

"Everything I suppose. We do not practice censorship. We transmit all the usual TV entertainment channels as well as educational and news services. They are well supplied with television receivers and can watch reruns of all the most loathsome programs and series. The theory being if we can stun their minds with televised crap they won't get up to more trouble."

"Does it work?"

"Possibly. But we do know that they are rated on top of the galactic viewing scale for uninterrupted hours in front of the gogglebox."

"You go there and take surveys?"

"Don't be stupid. Recorders are sealed into the chassis of each set. These can be tapped by satellite."

"So what we have here is a planet of murderous, belligerent, nutsy TV fans?"

"That's about the size of it."

I jumped to my feet, spilling dry crumbs of dead sandwiches onto the carpet. Raised my fists, and my voice, on high.

"That's it!"

Benbow blinked at me rapidly and scowled.

"What's it?"

"The answer. It is just the glimmering of an idea now—but I know that it will grow and expand into something incredible. I'm going to sleep on it and when I awake I will polish it and perfect it and describe it to you in detail."

"What is it?"

"Don't be greedy. All in good time."

# CHAPTER 4

The automated kitchen produced another stale sandwich, the machine was half-knackered and out of adjustment, along with a lukewarm cup of watery cocoa. I crunched and sipped gloomily, then found the bedroom down the hall. Air-conditioned of course—but the window wasn't sealed. I opened it and sniffed the cool night air. The moon was rising, to join the other three already up. Made for some interesting shadows. A leg over the windowsill, a drop into the garden—and I would be long gone before any alarm might go off.

And I would be dead in twenty-nine days. That little drink I had drunk in prison really concentrated my attention and guaranteed my loyalty. But could I pull this complicated operation off in that space of time?

Considering the consequences I had no choice. I sighed tremulously, closed the window and went to bed. It had been a very, very long day.

In the morning I had picked the lock on the control panel in the kitchen and was busy rewiring it when Admiral Benbow came in.

"May I inquire politely just what the hell you are doing?"

"Obviously trying to get this crook device to produce something other than stale cheese sandwiches. There!"

I slammed the panel shut and punched in a command. A cup of steaming coffee instantly appeared. Followed by a porcuswinewich, steaming and juicy. The Admiral nodded.

"I'll take this one—get another for yourself. Now tell me your plan."

I did. Mumbling through mouthfuls of breakfast.

"We are going to spend some credits out of the mountains of money that we have access to. First we plant some news items. I want interviews, reviews, gossip and more—all about the new pop group that is the hit of the galaxy."

He scowled and growled. "What pop group? What in hades are you talking about?"

"The planet-busting hit group called . . ."

"Called what?"

"I don't know. I haven't thought about it yet. Something way out and memorable. Or kinky." I smiled and raised an inspired finger. "I have it! Ready? The group is called . . . The Stainless Steel Rats!"

"Why?"

"Why not?"

The Admiral was not happy. His scowl turned to a snarl and he jabbed a judgmental finger at me. "More coffee. Then tell me what you are talking about or I will kill you."

"Temper, temper, Admiral. Remember the old blood pressure. What I am talking about is getting to Liokukae with all the equipment I need, along with some strongarmed help. We are going to form a group of musicians called The Stainless Steel Rats—"

"What musicians?"

"Me for one—and you are going to supply me with the rest. You did tell me that you were head of League Navy Security?"

"I did. I am."

"Then summon your troops. Get one of your techs to research all your field operators, all your rankings who have ever served in what passes for action in this civilized universe. The search will be a simple one because we want to know just one

single fact about all of them. Are they musically inclined? Can
they play a musical instrument, sing, dance, whistle or even
hum in tune? Get the list and we will have our band."

He nodded over his coffee. "You're beginning to make
sense. A pop group composed only of security agents. But it
will take time to put together, to organize, to rehearse."

"Why?"

"So it will sound good, you moron."

"Who could tell the difference? Have you ever listened to
country-and-coal-mining music? Or Aqua Regia and her Pluto-
nium Pals?"

"Point taken. So we get this group together and publicize
them well so all Liokukae knows about them—"

"And has heard their music—"

"And wants to hear more. On tour. Which is impossible.
The planet is quarantined."

"That is the beauty of my plan, Admiral. When the publicity peaks, and the fame of the group is galaxy-wide, that is
when the Rats will commit some crime so awful that they will
instantly be shipped off to this prison planet. Where they will
be received with great enthusiasm. And no suspicion. Where
they will investigate and find the alien artifact and get it back
so I can have the antidote. One other thing. Before we start
operations I will need three million Interstellar Credits. In
coins that have been newly minted here."

"No way," he snarled. "Funds will be supplied as
needed."

"You missed the point. That is my fee for conducting this
operation. All operating expenses are on top of that. Pay up—
or else."

"Or else what?"

"Or else I die in twenty-nine days and the operation dies
and you get a black mark on your service record."

Self-interest prodded him into an instant decision. "Why

not. Those financially overburdened academics can afford it and not even notice it. I'll get that list for you."

He unclipped his phone from his belt, shouted a multi-digit number into it, then barked some brief commands. Before I had finished my coffee the printer hummed to life in the office; sheets of paper began to pile up in the bin. We went through them and ticked off a number of possibilities. There were no names, just code numbers. When this was done I passed the list back to the Admiral.

"We'll need complete files on all the marked ones."

"That is classified and secret information."

"And you are the Admiral and you can get it."

"I'll get it—and censor it. There is no way I am going to let you know any details of my Security Department."

"Keep your secrets—I couldn't care less." Which was of course an outright lie. "Give them code names as well as numbers, conceal their identities. All I want to know is their musical abilities, and will they be any good in the field when the going gets rough."

This took a bit of time. I went for a long jog to loosen the muscles. Then, while my clothes were being zapped clean in the vacuum washer, I took a hot shower followed by a cold one. I made a mental note to get some more clothes soon—but not until this operation was up and running. There was no escaping that deadly clock that was ticking off the seconds to doomsday.

"Here is the list," the Admiral said when I entered the office. "No names, just numbers. Male agents are identified by the letter *A* and . . ."

"Let me guess—the females are *B*?"

A growl was his only response; he completely lacked any sense of humor. I flipped through the list. Slim pickings among the ladies who ran the gamut from B1 to B4. Pipe-organ player, not very likely, harmonica, tuba—and a singer.

"I'll need a photograph of B3. And what do these other entries after B1 mean? 19T, 908L, and such."

"Code," he said, grabbing the sheet away from me. "It translates as skilled in hand-to-hand combat, qualified marksman on hand weapons, six years in the field. And the rest is none of your business."

"Thanks, wonderful, you're a big help. I sure could use her —but not if she has to carry the pipe organ on her back. Now let us make some selections from the male list and get the photos coming. Except for this one, A19. No photograph—I just want him here soonest, in the flesh."

"Why?"

"Because he is a percussionist and plays a molecular-synthezier. Since I know next to nothing about music—he is going to teach me my job in this pickup band. A19 will show me the ropes, then record the numbers and set up the machines to play the different hunks of music. I'll just smile and press buttons. Speaking of machines—does your highly secret service have electronic repair facilities on this planet?"

"That is classified information."

"*Everything* about this operation is classified. But I'll still need to do some electronic work. Here or someplace else. All right?"

"Facilities will be made available."

"Good. And tell me—what is a gastrophone, or a bagpipe?"

"I haven't the slightest idea. Why?"

"Because they are listed here as musical skills or instruments or something. I'll need to know."

Lubricated by all the credits from the university, manned by the Admiral's minions, the machinery of my plan began to churn into high gear. The League did have an outpost on this planet—disguised as an interstellar shipping firm—which contained a fully equipped machine shop and electronic facilities.

The fact that they gave me full use of everything meant that it would undoubtedly vanish as soon as this operation was over. While the auditions were being arranged, agent A19 was sent for by the fastest transportation available. He appeared, slightly glassy-eyed, later that same afternoon.

"You are known to me only by the code reference A19. Could you give me a slightly better name to call you by? And it doesn't have to be your own."

He was a big man with a big jaw, which he rubbed as he kicked his brain into action. "Zach—that's my cousin's name. Call me Zach."

"Right on, Zach. You have quite a musical record."

"You betcha. I worked my way through college playing in the band. Still do a gig or two from time to time."

"Then you have the job. You must now sally forth with an open checkbook and buy the best, most expensive and complex hunks of electronic music making that you can find. And they have to be the most compact and microminiaturized ones going. Bring them back and I'll make it all smaller since everything we bring with us has to be carried on our backs. If you can't find it on this planet use galactic mail order. Spend! The more you spend the better."

His eyes glowed with musical fervor. "Do you mean that?"

"Absolutely. Check with Admiral Benbow who will authorize all expenses. Go!"

He went, and the auditions began. I draw a veil over the more repulsive details of the next two days. Apparently musical ability and military service were mutually incompatible for the most part. I whittled away and the list grew smaller with great rapidity. I had hoped for a large band—now it appeared that I had a tiny combo.

"This is it, Admiral," I said, passing over the abbreviated list. "We will have to make up in quality what we lack in quantity. It is going to be me and these three others."

He frowned. "Will it be enough?"

"Going to have to be. The discards may be great operators but I will dream about their sounds for years. In my nightmares. So take the survivors aside, tell them about me and the assignment. I'll meet them after lunch in the audition room."

I was setting glasses and bottles of refreshment on the table when the four of them trooped in. In step!

"First lesson!" I shouted. "Think civilian. Anything that even resembles the military will get us all quickly dead. Now— have you all talked to the Admiral? Everyone is nodding, good, good. Nod again if you agree to take orders from me and no one else. Even better. Now I will introduce you to each other. I have been forbidden knowledge of your real names and positions so I have invented some. Let us now begin the world anew. The gentleman on your left, code name Zach, is a professional musician and is tutoring me in my new skills. He will be of utmost help in getting this project off the ground. I am Jim and I will soon be able to play the electronic gadgetry and lead this group. The young lady in your presence, now named Madonette, is a contralto of great talent and our lead singer. Let's give her a big hand."

Slowly at first, then louder and jollier, they clapped until I lifted a hand to stop them. They were an uptight lot and I had to get them a lot looser. Madonette was fair of skin and dark of hair; a tall and solid girl and quite attractive, she smiled and waved in return.

"Good beginning gang. Now you last two guys, you're the rest of this group, Floyd and Steengo. Floyd is the tall and skinny guy with the artificial beard—he is growing a real replacement for it, but we needed one now for the publicity pix. The miracle workers of hirsutical science have developed an antidipilatorisational agent that stimulates hair growth. So he will grow a fine beard in three days. In addition to growing hair he plays a number of wind instruments which are, if you don't know, a historic family of musical instruments into which one blows strongly to emit sounds. He comes from a distant planet named Och'aye, which is perhaps galaxy-famous for its other native son Angus McSwiney, founder of the McSwiney chain of automated eateries. Floyd plays an instrument whose antecedents are lost in the mists of time and at times I wish they had stayed there. Floyd, a quick tune on the bagpipe if you please."

I had heard it before so was slightly more prepared as he opened the case and removed an apparatus that looked like a large and bulging spider with many black legs. He slung it about him, puffed strongly and pumped furiously on the spider's abdomen with his arm. I looked at the others and admired their horrified expressions as the screams of mortally wounded animals filled the room.

"Enough!" I shouted and the last slaughtered pig moaned away into deathly silence. "I don't know if this instrument will be featured in our recitals—but you must admit that it does draw attention. Last, and certainly not least, is Steengo. Who after he left the service became quite adept on the fiddelino. Steengo, a demonstration if you please."

Steengo smiled paternally at us and waved. He had gray hair and an impressive paunch. I was concerned about his age and general fitness but the Admiral, after secretly scanning the records, reassured me that Steengo's health was A-OK, that he worked out regularly and, other than a tendency towards slight overweight, he was fit for field conditions. I shrugged—since there was little else I could do. The records revealed that he had taken up the instrument after retirement from active duty; with talent in such short supply I had had the veterans' records searched as well. When approached he was more than happy to get back into harness. The fiddelino had two necks and twenty strings and sounded rather jolly in a plucking scratching way that everyone seemed to enjoy. Steengo bowed graciously to acknowledge the applause.

"That's it then. You have just met The Stainless Steel Rats. Any questions?"

"Yes," Madonette said, and all eyes turned her way. "What is the music that we will be playing?"

"Good question—and I think I have a good answer. Research into contemporary music reveals a great variety of rhythms and themes. Some of them pretty bad, like country-and-steel-mill music. Some with a certain charm like the Chipperinos and their flock of singing birds. But we need something new and different. Or old and different as long as no one has heard the music in a few thousand years. For our inspiration I have had the music department at Galaksia Universitato research their most ancient data bases. Millennia have passed since this music was last heard. Usually with good reason."

I held up a handful of recordings. "These are the survivors of a grueling test I put them through. If I could listen for more than fifteen seconds I made a copy. We will now refine the process even more. Anything we can bear for thirty seconds goes into the second round."

I popped one of the tiny black chips into the player and sat back. Atonal musical thunder rumbled over us and a soprano with a voice like a pregnant porcuswine assailed our ears. I popped the recording out, ground it under my heel, then went on to the next one.

By late afternoon our eyes were red-rimmed with tears, our ears throbbing, our brains numbed and throbbing as well.

"Is that enough for the moment?" I asked sweetly and my answer was a chorus of groans. "Right. On the way in here I noticed that right next door is a drinking parlor by the name of Dust on Your Tonsils. I can only assume that is a little joke and they intend to wash the dust from their clients' tonsils. Shall we see if that is true?"

"Let's go!" Floyd said and led the exodus.

"A toast," I said when the drinks had arrived. We lifted our glasses. "To The Stainless Steel Rats—long may they play!"

They cheered and drank, then laughed and called for another round. It was all going to work out hunky-dory I thought.

Then why was I so depressed?

# CHAPTER 5

I was depressed because it was really a pretty madcap plan. The idea had been to allow a week for our publicity to peak, for some musical awards to be made—then the crime had to occur. In that brief period we were not only going to have to find some music, but we would have to rehearse the stuff and hopefully gain at least a moderate level of ability. Some chance. We were cutting it too fine. We needed some more help.

"Madonette, a question." I sipped some more beer first. "I must admit to an abysmal ignorance of the mechanics of making music. Is there someone who sort of makes up the tunes, then writes down the stuff that everyone is going to play?"

"You're talking about a composer and an arranger. They could be one and the same—but it is usually better to divide up the jobs."

"Can we get one or both of them? Zach, as the closest thing to a professional here—do you have any ideas?"

"Shouldn't be too hard. All we have to do is contact GAS-CAP."

"Gascap? You want to fill the tank on a groundcar?"

"Not gascap. GASCAP. An acronym for the Galactic Society of Composers Artists and Players. There is a lot of unemployment in music and we should be able to locate some really competent people."

"Good as done. I'll get the Admiral on it at once."

"Impossible," he growled in his usually friendly fashion. "No civilians, no outsiders. This is a secret operation all the way."

"It is now—but it goes public in seven days. All we do is invent a cover story. Say that the group is being organized to make a holofilm. Or as a publicity stunt by a big firm. Like maybe McSwineys wants to change their image, go upmarket. Get rid of Blimey McSwiney and his alcoholic red nose, use our pop group instead. But it must be done—and at once."

It was. The next day an anorexic and pallid young man was brought to our rehearsal studio. Zach whispered in my ear. "I recognize him—that's Barry Moyd Shlepper. He wrote a pop musical a couple of years back, "Don't Fry for Me, Angelina." He hasn't had a success since."

"I remember it. The show about the cook who marries the dictator."

"That's the one."

"Welcome, Barry, welcome," I said walking over and shaking his bony hand. "My name is Jim and I'm in charge around here."

"Rooty-toot, man, rooty-toot," he said.

"And a rooty-toot to you as well." I could see where we would have to learn the argot of the musical world if our plan were to succeed. "Now—was this operation explained to you?"

"Like maybe sort of. A new recording company starting up with plenty of bucknicks to blow. Financing some new groups to get the operation off the ground."

"That's it. You're in charge of the music. Let me show you what we have and you put it into shape."

I gave him earphones and the player: I couldn't bear listening to these dreadful compositions yet another time. He plugged in the cubes one by one and, impossible as it was to believe, his pallid skin grew even paler. He worked his way through them all. Sighed tremulously, took off the earphones and brushed the tears from his eyes.

"You want like my honest and truly opinion?"

"Nothing less."

"Well then, like to break it to you gently, this stuff really sucks. Insufflates. Implodes."

"Can you do better?"

"My cat can do better. And scratch dirt over it."

"Then you are unleashed. Begin!"

There was little else I could do until the music was written, rehearsed, recorded. While all the others would play their instruments and sing, my work would be limited to throwing the switch before each piece. Then all of Zach's drums, cymbals, horns, bells and molecular-synthezier effects would burst forth from the loudspeakers in full gallop. While this was happening I would throw switches that did nothing, tinkle the keys on a disconnected keyboard. So while they got the music going I looked into the special effects.

This required watching recordings of all of the most popular groups, bands and soloists. Some of it was enjoyable, some horribly dreadful, all of it too loud. In the end I turned off the sound and watched the laser beams, exploding fireworks and physical acrobatics. I made sketches, mumbled to myself a lot, spent a great deal of the university's money.

And built an incredible amount of complicated circuitry into the existing electronics. Reluctantly, the Admiral produced the extras I asked for and I modified everything in the machine shop. It was altogether a satisfactory and fulfilling week. I also prodded the Admiral until he produced the promised payment of three million credits.

"Most kind," I said, jingling the six glowing five-hundred-thousand-credit coins. "A decent fee for a decent job done."

"You better put them in a bank vault before they go missing," was his surly advice.

"Of course. A capital idea!"

A singularly stupid idea. Banks were for robbing and for the tax authorities to keep track of. So first I went into the machine shop where I did some crafty metalwork before I packed wrapped and labeled the coins. Then I went for a walk and, as a precaution, I exercised all of my considerable talents at avoiding observation to shake off any possible tails the Admiral had put on me. I was risking my life—in more ways than one!—for this money. If I came out of it all in one piece I wanted to have it waiting.

I finally reached a small country post office, selected at random, some distance from the city. It was manned by a near-sighted gentleman of advanced years.

"Spatial express and insured for offplanet delivery. That ain't gonna be cheap young feller."

"Do it, daddy-o, do it. I've got the gilt." He blinked and I translated back to his native language. "Payment is not a problem, dear sir. You must assure me that this gets to Professor Van Diver at the Galaksia Universitato at once. He is expecting these historical documents."

I had already spaciofaxed the professor that I was sending him some personal possessions, that he should please hold on to them until I came and picked them up. In case he got curious the contents were sealed in an armored case that would take a diamond drill to open. I was betting that his curiosity would not go that far. My package vanished into the mailchute and I went back to work.

At the end of the sixth day we were all pretty exhausted. Barry Moyd Shlepper had stayed up for two nights running, cold towels wrapped around his head, fortified by trebcaff coffee, putting together some musical numbers from the archaic junk. He proved to be a good hand at theft—or adaptation as he liked to call it. The group had rehearsed, recorded, then rehearsed some more. I had concentrated on costumes, props and effects and was almost satisfied.

After one last break I called my troops together. "You will be pleased to know that we will now give our first public performance." This produced the expected groans and shrill cries of complaint and I waited until they had died down.

"I know how you feel—and I feel the same way too. I think that the blues number, 'I'm All Alone,' is our best piece. You know we have had a lot of help from the staff here and I think we owe it to them to see what we all have done. I've invited something like thirty of them and they should be here soon."

Right on cue the door opened and the suspicious public employees filed in, each carrying a folding chair. Admiral Benbow led the way; his flag officer carried two chairs. Zach supervised the seating arrangements and our cavernous rehearsal studio became a theater for the first time. We retreated to the podium where I dimmed the houselights, then hit myself and my electronic gear with a baby spot.

"Ladies, gentlemen, guests. We have all worked hard this last week and in the name of The Stainless Steel Rats I would like to thank you."

I hit a switch and my amplified voice echoed Thank You, Thank You. Overlaid by a growing crescendo of drums and ending with a crack of thunder and a few realistic lightning bolts. I could see by their wide eyes and dropped jaws that I had their attention.

"For our first number the melodious Madonette will render heart-rendingly the tragically lonely—'I'm All Alone'!"

At this the colored kliegs burst down on us, revealing our pink-sequined skintight costumes in all their iridescent glory. As we played the opening bars of the theme the lights concentrated on Madonette, whose costume had more flesh than fabric and seemed to be deeply appreciated. After a last whistle of wind and crash of thunder and lighting she extended her lovely arms to the audience and sang:

> *Here I am—and I'm all alone—*
> *No one calls on the telephone.*
> *I look around—and what do I see?*
> *There's no one here but me—me—me.*
> *Me—me—me*
> *That's all I see—*
> *I'm all alone*
> *Just*
> > *me*
> > > *me*
> > > > *me . . .*

This was all done to the accompaniment of holographic shaking trees, storm clouds and other spooky effects. The music wailed as Madonette seguidillad into the rest of the song.

> *I'm all alone and it's very dark—*
> *I sneak out the window to the park.*
> > *The wind blows hard and the tree limbs wave—*
> *And I'm right before an open grave!*
> *When I try to run and try to flee—*
> *But I KNOW they're out there after me!*
> *I sit and cry and I know that's right—*
> > *Because the sun comes up—*
> > *It's the end of the night . . .*

With a last wail and a writhe of purple fog the sun rose majestically behind us and the music trickled to an end.

The silence stretched and stretched—until it was finally broken by a tumultuous applause.

"Well gang," I said, "it looks like we have done it. Or as Barry Moyd says it looks like we are but really rooty-getooty!"

On the seventh day we did not rest. After a final round of rehearsals I called an early break. "Get some racktime. Pack your bags. The music and props are ready to go. We ship out at midnight. Transportation to the spaceport leaves here an hour earlier—so don't be late."

They shuffled out wearily with dragging feet. The Admiral stamped in as they left, with Zach trailing in his wake.

"This agent informs me that all preparations have been made and you are ready to embark." I could only nod agreement.

"Wish I could go with you," Zach said.

"You set it all up—you have our thanks for that. Now get going."

He numbed my fingers with his handshake and the door closed behind him.

The Admiral's smile had all of the warmth of a striking snake. "Drug Enforcement has come up with a crime so awful that it means an instant sentence to Liokukae."

"That's nice—what is it?"

"Misuse of a highly refined and expensive drug called baksheesh. You and the rest of the musicians have been caught smuggling it and are addicted to it. There is a medical cure for the addiction that leaves the victim weak and vibrating for a number of days. This should give you a little time to look around before you have to play your first concert. The press release has already gone out about your capture and your sentence to prison hospital for the criminally doped. The natives of Liokukae will not be surprised at all when you arrive there. Questions?"

"A big one. Has the communication been set up?"

"Yes. The coded radio built into your jaw can reach the receiver at the entrance terminal from any place on the planet. It will be manned all of the time and an officer will be listening in on all communication. Your contact on the ground will give you what aid he can before you go out of the sealed terminal. Then he will move to the spacecruiser *Remorseless* in orbit above, which will also monitor your radio. We can hit any-where on the planet in a maximum of eleven minutes. Send the signal when you have found the artifact and the space marines will be there. Report at a minimum of once a day. Location and results of your investigation."

"Just in case we get blown away and you have to send in the second team?"

"Exactly. More questions?"

"One. Going to wish us luck?"

"No. Don't believe in it. Make your own."

"Gee, thanks, you really are all heart."

He turned and stamped away and the door swung shut behind him. Fatigue washed through me and black depression hit just one more time. Why was I doing this?

To stay alive of course. Twenty-two days more before my curtain fell for the final performance.

# CHAPTER 6

The Faster Than Light voyage aboard the good ship *Remorse-less* was blessedly brief. Being surrounded by the military has always had a deleterious effect on my morale. We had a solid day of rehearsal, some bad food, a good night's rest, followed the next day by a very non-alcoholic party—since the Navy was remorselessly teetotal. Then, a few hours before we were to meet the shuttle, the medics gave us the injections that were to simulate the aftereffects of our drug treatment.

I think I would have preferred the treatment. I didn't mind seeing my last meal go by for a second time; it had been pretty bad and I would not miss it. But the shakes and shivers were something else again. And all of my vibrating and stumbling co-musicians had eyeballs as red as fire. I dared not look in the mirror for fear of what I would see there.

Steengo was gray and drawn and looked a hundred years old. I felt a quick blast of guilt for dragging him out of retirement. Said guilt fading instantly when I thought about my own problems.

"Do I look as bad as you do?" Floyd said in a hoarse voice, his new-grown beard black against his parchment skin.

"I hope not," I husked in return. Madonette reached over and patted my shaking hand in what might have been a maternal way.

"It will be all right on the night, Jim. Just you wait and see."

I did not feel filial in return since I was rapidly developing a crush on her that I hoped I disguised. I growled something or other and stumbled away to the heads where I could be alone with my misery. Even this did not work for the speaker in the ceiling rustled ominously—then crashed out Admiral Benbow's voice.

"Now hear this. All Stainless Steel Rats will assemble at debarkation station twelve in two minutes. We are now in parking orbit. One minute and fifty-eight seconds. One minute and . . ."

I slammed out into the passageway to escape his voice but it followed me as I fled. I was the last to arrive and I collapsed and joined the others where they slumped on the deck beside our backpacks. The Admiral appeared suddenly behind me like a bad dream and roared his command.

"Attention! On your feet you slovenly crew!"

"Never!" I shouted even louder in a cracked voice. Rolling over to pull the swaying bodies back to the deck.

"Begone foul military fiend! We are musicians, civilians, medically reformed drug addicts and we must think and feel that way. Someday, if we live, you may have some of us back at your military mercy. But not now. Leave us in peace and wait for my reports."

He snarled a rich naval oath—but had the brains to turn on his heel and vanish. There was a ragged cheer from my companions which made me feel slightly less sordid. The silence after this was unbroken, except for the occasional groan, until distant motors whirred and the inner lock swung majestically open. A keen clipboard-bearing naval officer stepped through.

"Landing party for Liokukae?"

"All present, all ill. Send a working party for our gear."

He muttered into his lapel microphone, reached to the back of his belt to unclip a pair of handcuffs. Which he promptly snapped onto my wrists.

"Whasha?" I blurted incoherently. Blinking down at the cuffs.

"Don't give me a hard time, you drug-pushing addict, and I won't give you one. You may be a big man out there in the galaxy, but here you are just one more sentenced crook. Who is going to carry his own pack—no working party for the likes of you."

I opened my mouth to verbally assassinate him. Then closed it. It had been my idea that our mission be known to the minimum few. He obviously wasn't one of them. I groaned to my feet and stumbled into the airlock dragging my gear after me; the others following in like condition. The orbital shuttle ship was grim and cheerless. The hard metal seats snapped clamps on our ankles when we sat down; no dancing in the aisles this trip. We watched in silence as our backpacks were thrown into a storage bin, then looked up at the big screen on the front bulkhead. Lots of stars. They rotated and the bulk of *Remorseless* swam into sight, grew smaller and dropped behind as the engines fired. Then the pickup turned so that the growing bulk of the planet could be seen and we were treated to a scratchy and static-filled ancient recording of martial music. This died away and was replaced by a male speaker with a repulsive nasal whine.

"Now hear this, prisoners. This is a one-way trip. You will have resisted all efforts at adjustment that would have fitted you to live peacefully in our humane and civilized society . . ."

"Blow it out your rocket tubes!" Steengo snarled, running his fingers through his gray hair, perhaps to see if it was still there. I would have nodded agreement with his snarl only my head hurt too much.

". . . brought upon yourselves by your own efforts. Upon landing you will be escorted by armed guards to the gates of the landing station. Your restraints will be removed and you will be given an orientation booklet, a canteen of distilled water, as well as a week's supply of concentrated survival rations. During that week you will look for small trees bearing hard fruit. These are the polpettone trees and a source of nourishment for all. Their fruit is the result of careful gene mutation and transplant, rich in animal protein. They should not be eaten raw because of the chance of trichinosis, but should be baked or boiled. You must remember . . ."

I wanted to remember nothing he said so I tuned him out. I tried to reassure myself that the normal condemned passenger on this flight must have done something pretty gruesome to deserve this fate. I wasn't convinced. Despite millennia of civilization man's inhumanity to man persisted whenever an opportunity presented itself.

The imaged clouds blew by and a massive five-sided building appeared on the screen. I supposed they called it the Pentagon.

"In a few moments we will be landed inside the walls of the Pentagon debarkation station. Remain seated until you are ordered to rise. Follow instructions and your passage will be made that much easier . . ."

I would like to make his passage easier! Then I relaxed and opened my fists. Very soon we would be away from weary wardens and on our own. That was the moment to be prepared for.

We shuffled out in silence, down the gangway—which surely should have been a gangplank—and into the thick-walled Pentagon. To be greeted by yet another naval officer, grim-faced and gray-haired, wearing dark glasses.

"Take the prisoners to Interview nine at once."

The petty officer of our guard protested. "Not regulation, sir. They have to—"

"You have to close your gob. Look at these orders. Do as instructed. You do enjoy being a petty officer?"

"Yes, *sir*! Prisoners this way!"

The officer came in after us, closed and locked the door, smiled at us warmly and said "Shut up" companionably. He then walked around the room with what I recognized as being a state of the art communication detector. I couldn't imagine who would want to bug the room here at the end of the universe—but he was in charge. Satisfied he put the detector away and turned to face us and handed me a key.

"You can take the cuffs off while we are in this room. I am Captain Tremearne and I am your contact here. Welcome to Liokukae." He took off the dark glasses and smiled at us and waved us to the chairs. I could see now that a wicked scar slashed across his face and the bridge of his nose. He was blind. But could undoubtedly see fine with the electronic replacement eyes that had been fitted. They were gold-plated and gave him a highly interesting appearance.

"I am the only one here in the Pentagon who knows the real nature of your assignment here. You are all volunteers and I would like to thank you. Help yourself to refreshments because that is the last kind word you are going to hear for quite a while."

"What is it like out there?" I asked, touching the seal on a chilled container of beer and taking a life-reviving swig. There were fresh sandwiches and hot swinedogs there as well and my companions all dived in. I joined them, but not before I had opened a concealed drawer in my synthezier and taken out some necessary items.

"What's life like on this planet? Grim—and worse than grim, Jim. In the centuries that Liokukae has been used as a societal galactic wastebin there has been a rather deadly shaking down. Different cultures have been formed here as like found like. Or violent men forced violent solutions upon weaker men. One of the most stable of these has been developed right outside the Pentagon. They call themselves the

Machmen. Man is strong, woman weak, virility rules, strength through strength, I'm sure that you know the kind of thing. The top dog in this kennel, whom I am sure you will be meeting soon, is named Svinjar."

"Are these weirdos what the psych books call male chauvinist pigs?" I asked. He nodded.

"Absolutely correct. So do your best to keep Madonette out of sight. And practice walking on your toes and flaring your nostrils at the same time. If you can't think of anything else to do crook your arm and admire your biceps."

"Sounds a paradise," she frowned.

"Won't be too bad if you watch your step. They like to be entertained—since they haven't enough brains to entertain themselves. Very big on jugglers, duels, arm wrestling."

"What about music?" Steengo asked.

"Fine—as long as it is loud, martial and not sentimental."

"We'll do our best," I said. "But it is a group called the Fundamentaloids that I want to look for."

"Of course. As you have been told the spacer with the archeological expedition landed in their area of operation. I led the rescue party that took the expedition members out of here—which is why I am your contact now. The Fundamentaloids are nomads, as well as being pretty narrow-minded and obnoxious. I tried to keep things calm with them. Didn't work. In the end I narcgassed the lot and went in and pulled the scientists out. I didn't find out about the missing artifact until much later when we were offplanet and they were conscious again and the excitement had cooled down. By this time the group that had grabbed them had moved on and the trail got cold. Nothing more I could do at the time but report it. It's all in your hands now."

"Thanks much. Can't you at least point out to me on the map where they are?"

"Wish I could—but they're nomads."

"Wonderful." I smiled insincerely. Twenty days to deadline. *Deadline!* it would be. I shook off the dark feelings just
one more time, looked around at my band.

"Ask questions if you have any because this is your last
chance," Tremearne said.

"Do you have a map?" I asked. "I would like to know just
what we have to face when we go out there."

Tremearne reached to the holo projector and switched it
on. A three-dimensional contour map appeared in midair over
the table. "This is a fair-sized continent as you can see. There
are other continents on this planet, some inhabited, but they
have no contact with this one. The artifact has to be somewhere here."

That really simplifies things, I thought to myself. Only one
continent to search and about three weeks to do it in. I shook
off the depression that was depressing my depression.

"Do you know who and what are out there?"

"We have a good idea. We plant bugs where we can, fly
spyeyes pretty often." He tapped the plain at the center of the
continent. "Here is the Pentagon with the Machmen close by
outside it. The Fundamentaloids could be anywhere here on
the plains depending on the season. It is subtropical most of
the year, but rainfall varies. They have herds of sheots, a very
hardy ruminant, some kind of cross between a sheep and a
goat. Now over here in the foothills is the closest thing that
passes for civilization in these parts. An agricultural society
with light industry that looks almost decent until you get close.
There is a central city, right here, surrounded by farms. They
mine and smelt silver and produce a coin called a fedha. It is
the only currency on the planet and is used by almost everyone." He pulled a heavy bag out of a drawer and dropped it
onto the table. "As you can well imagine they are easy enough
to forge. In fact ours have more silver than the originals.
Here's a supply for you. I suggest that you share it around and
hide it well. A lot of types out there would be happy to kill you

for just one of these. The people who mine the silver call their city Paradise—which is about as far away from a true description as you can get. Stay away from them—if you possibly can."

"I'll try to remember that. And I want to copy this into memory in my computer. Here."

I took off the small black metal skull that hung on a chain around my neck. When I squeezed it the eyes glowed greenly and a pressure-sensitive holoscreen blinked into being; I copied the map, thought about what Tremearne had said—and realized for the first time what a sinkhole we were being dropped into. I had another question.

"So everyone out there is a nutcase or a weirdo of some kind?"

"The ones that were sent here for various crimes are. The ones who were born here grow up and fit in just as well."

"And you feel no compassion for them? Doomed by an accident of birth to existence in this world-wide spittoon."

"I certainly do—and I am glad to hear you express yourself so clearly on the subject. I never even heard of this world until the emergency. I got the professors off safely then looked around. Which is why I now head the committee that is working to clean up the operation here on Liokukae. It has been ignored for too long by too many stupid politicians. I took this assignment to see for myself. Your reports to me, along with your complete report when you return, will be just what we need to make this prison world a thing of the past."

"If you mean that, Captain, I'm on your side. But I hope you are not feeding a line of old cagal just to get the job done."

"You have my word on it."

I sure hoped that he was telling the truth.

"I have a question," Floyd said. "How do we contact the Captain here if we need some help or such?"

"You don't—I do." I tapped my jaw. "I've got a micro-

communicator implant here. Small enough to be powered by
the oxygen in my blood. But powerful enough to be picked up
by the big receivers in the Pentagon. So even if all of our
goods are stolen—they can't get my jaw. So, I suggest strongly,
we stick together at all times. I can talk with Tremearne
through this thing, get suggestions and advice. But no physical
contact or our cover is blown. If he has to pull us out the
mission is over—whether we have the artifact or not. So let us
be strong, guys and girl, and self sufficient. It's a human jungle
out there."

"No truer words ever spoken," Tremearne said grimly. "If
no one else has any questions put the cuffs back on and you're
out of here."

"Hell yes," Steengo said, climbing to his feet. "Let's get it
over with."

Our packs were waiting for us in front of a massive and
bolt-studded door. There were four shoddy little plastic bags
as well, which probably contained our iron rations and water.
An orientation booklet was tucked into each one. A backup
force of guards with stunguns and porcuswine prods stomped
up and glared obnoxiously while our manacles were removed.

"In there," the petty officer ordered, pointing to the ante-
room in front of the exit portal. "Inner door is closed and
sealed before the outside one opens. You got only one way to
go. Or stay in the room if you are tired of living. After five
minutes the outer door closes and nerve gas is pumped in
through those vents up there."

"I don't believe you!" I snapped.

His smile was without warmth. "Then why don't you just
hang around and find out?"

I raised my fist and he hurriedly jumped back. The porcuswine prods sparkled in my direction. I raised my finger to
them in the intergalactic gesture that is as old as time, turned
and walked away from them following the others. There was a

creak and a thud from behind us as the door swung shut, but I did not turn to look. The future, whatever it contained, lay just ahead.

We helped each other on with our packs, swaying dizzily with the effort. There was the thud of withdrawn bolts from inside the door, the growl of straining motors as it started to open.

Unconsciously we drew together as we turned to face the unknown.

# CHAPTER 7

A splatter of rain blew in through the opening door. Welcome to sunny, holiday Liokukae. Which opened wider to reveal the group of very ugly-looking individuals who were waiting outside. They were dressed in an astounding variety of clothing—it looked like all the donations to charity in the entire galaxy had been sent here—and they all had two things in common. They were heavily armed with a mixture of clubs, swords, maces and axes. And they all looked very angry.

Just about what I had expected; I chomped down on the Blastoff capsule I had put in my mouth. I had never thought much of the weaklings-recovering-from-treatment plan and had palmed this pill in case it were needed. It was.

A wave of energy and power washed through me as the mixture of powerful chemicals, uppers, stimulants, adrenalins, swept away all the fatigue and shakes. Power! Power! Power! I swayed forward on tiptoes as Tremearne had advised, flaring my nostrils at the same time.

A great bearded lout swinging a crude but serviceable sword glared down at me. I glared back, noting that not only did his eyes meet in the middle but that his hairline also started at his eyebrows. When he shouted at me his breath frightened me more than he did.

"You dere, little boy. Gimme what you carrying. You all drop what you got or you get it."

"No one tell me what to do unless he can beat me, you illiterate cretin," I shouted back. The macho showdown with these macho mothers would have to take place sooner or later. Sooner was better.

He roared angrily at the insults, even though he could not understand them, and swung up the sword. I sneered.

"Big coward kill little man with sword when little man got no ax." I gave him two fingers to doubly amplify my feelings.

I hoped my simple syntax fitted the local linguistic profile because I wanted to make sure they all understood me. They must have, because Pigbreath dropped his sword and jumped towards me. I swung off my pack and stepped out into the mud. He had his arms out, fingers snapping, ready to grab and crush.

I ducked under them, tripped him as he went by to splat down into a puddle. He rose up, angrier than ever, balled his fists and came on more warily this time.

I could have finished it then and there and made life easier. But I had to display a bit of skill first so his mates wouldn't think that his downfall had been an accident. I blocked his punch, grabbed and twisted his arm, then ran him into the wall with a satisfactory crunch.

The blood from his nose did not improve his temper. Nor did my flying kick that numbed one of his legs, a stab with my knee that crumpled the other. Legless, he dropped to his knees, then crawled towards me on all fours. By this time even the dullest of the audience knew who had won this fight. So I grabbed him by the hair and pulled him up, hit his throat with the edge of my hand and let him keep going backwards, splatting down unconscious in the mud. I picked up his discarded sword, tested the edge with my thumb—jumped about so suddenly and menacingly that the armed men stepped away without thinking. I kept the momentum going.

"I got sword now. You want it, you die for it. Or maybe the smart bloke one of you what takes me to your boss,

Svinjar. Guy what does dat gets this sword for free. Any takers?"

The novelty of the offer and their inherent greed warded off any attack for the moment.

"Get out of there and get behind me," I called over my shoulder. "And do your best to radiate obnoxious intolerance." Growling and gnashing their teeth my merry band emerged and lined up at my back.

"You give me sword I take you Svinjar," an exceedingly hairy and musclebound specimen said. He was armed only with a wooden club so his greed was understandable.

"You take me Svinjar *then* you get sword. Move it."

There was hesitation, dark looks, muttering. I swished the sword under their noses so they had to step back again. "I got something real nice in my pack for Svinjar. You betcha he kill any bloke stop him grabbing it soonest."

Threats penetrated where blandishments hadn't and we all moved off into the rainstorm. Along muddy tracks between collapsing hovels, to a small hill with a largish building made of logs, their bark still on, gracing the summit. I swung the sword so no one came too close, followed my guide up a stony path to the entrance with my weary musicians stumbling after. I was feeling a bit guilty about taking the Blastoff capsule. But things had developed too quickly to get some to the others. I stopped at the entrance and waved them through.

"In we go, safe haven at last. Take one of these as you pass and chomp it instantly. It is a super-upper that will restore you to the world of the living."

My club-bearing guide pushed inside and hurried past the groups of men who lolled about the large room, to the man in the great stone chair next to the fireplace. "You my boss, boss Svinjar. We bring them like you say." He swung about and stamped over to me. "Now you give sword."

"Sure. Fetch."

I threw it out the door into the rain, heard a yipe of pain as it bounced off one of his gang. He ran after it as I walked over and stood before the stone throne.

"You my boss, boss Svinjar. These guys my band. Make good music you betcha."

He looked me up and down coldly, a big man with big muscles—as well as a big belly that hung over his belt. Tiny piggy eyes peered out through the thicket of bristly gray hair and beard. The pommel of a sword projected from a niche in the stone chair and he touched it with his fingers, slipping it out then letting it fall back.

"Why are you talking in that obnoxiously obscene patois?"

"I do beg your pardon." I bowed deprecatingly. "I was addressed in that manner and assumed it was the local dialect."

"It is—but only among the uneducated imbeciles who were born here. Since you weren't, don't offend my sensibility again. Are you the musicians that got into deep cagal?"

"Word sure spreads fast."

He waved his hand at the 3D set against the wall and I felt my eyes bulge. It was a solid metal block with an armored glass face—with the aerial under the glass. A handle stuck out one side.

"Our jailers are most generous in their desire that we be entertained at all times. They distribute these in great numbers. Unbreakable, eternal—and four hundred and twelve channels."

"What powers it?"

"Slaves," he said and reached out a toe to prod the nearest one. The slave groaned and climbed to his feet, stumbled over, clanking his chains as he went, and began to turn the handle on the internal generator. The thing burst to life with a commercial for industrial strength cat food.

"Enough!" Svinjar ordered and the meows faded and died.

"You and your companions kept the news channels alive. When they said crime and hospital treatment I was rather convinced they meant here. Ready to play?"

"The Stainless Steel Rats are always at the service of those in control. Which, in this case, I assume is you."

"You assume right. A concert it is—and now. We haven't had any live entertainment here since the cannibalistic magician died of infection after being bitten by accident in the heat of passion. Begin."

By necessity all our gear had to be compact. The fist-sized loudspeakers contained holoprojectors that blew their image up to room size.

"All right guys," I called out. "Let's set up by the back wall. No costumes for this first gig and we'll start with 'The Swedish Monster from Outer Space.' "

This was one of our more impressive numbers. It had been found in one of the most ancient data bases, the lyric written in a long-lost language called Svensk or Svedish or something like that. After much electronic scratching about, one of the computers in the language department at the university had been able to translate it. But this lyric was so dreadful that we threw it away and sang it in the original which was far more interesting.

*Ett fasanfullt monster med rumpan bar*
*kryper in till en jungfru sa rar.*

There was more like this and Madonette belted it out at full volume to the accompaniment of my syncopated soundtrack, with Floyd knocking himself out on his blower-powered bagpipe. Steengo plucked at a tiny harp—whose holographic image stretched up to the ceiling. Sound filled and reverberated through the great chamber and dust was jarred loose from the log walls.

I don't think that this tune would make the galactic top ten
—but it sure went down well here in endsville. Particularly
when it ended with an atomic mushroom cloud that grew to
room size—along with the best the amplifiers could do to simulate the atomic explosion itself. The part of the audience that
wasn't collapsed on the floor had fled shrieking into the rain. I
took out my earplugs and heard the light clapping of approval.
I bowed in Svinjar's direction.

"A pleasant *divertimento*—but the next time you play it I
would appreciate a little less *forza* in the finale and a little more
*riposo*."

"Your slightest wish is our command."

"For a young and simple-looking lad you learn fast. How
come you were caught pushing drugs?"

"It's a long story—"

"Shorten it. To one word if possible."

"Money."

"Understandable. Then the music business isn't that
good?"

"It smells like one of your bully-boys. If you can stay up
there with the big ones, fine. But we slipped from the top
notch some time ago. What with recording fees, agents' com-
missions, kickbacks and bribes we were quickly going bust.
Steengo and Floyd have been snorting back baksheesh for
years. They started selling it to support the habit. It's nice
stuff. End of story."

"Or beginning of a new one. Your singer, what's her
name?" He smiled a very unwholesome smile as he looked
over at Madonette. I groped for inspiration. Came up with the
best I could do at such short notice.

"You mean my wife, Madonette . . ."

"Wife? How inconvenient. I am sure that something can
be done about that, though not exactly at this moment. Your
arrival is, to say the least, most timely. Fits in with what you

might call a general plan of action I was considering. For the general good of the populace."

"Indeed," I said, controlling my enthusiasm for any plan of his that might be forthcoming.

"Yes, indeed. A concert for the public. Barbecues and free drinks. The public will see Svinjar as a benefactor of the first order. I gather that you are prepared to play a benefit performance?"

"That's what we are here for."

Among other things that we are here for, Svinjar old chubkin. But the longest journey begins with but a single step.

# CHAPTER 8

"I'm not happy about the way this operation is going," I said unhappily. Spooning up the almost tasteless gruel that appeared to be the staff of life in this place.

"Who's arguing?" Steengo said, looking suspiciously into his own bowl of food. "This stuff not only looks like glue—it tastes like it."

"It will stick to your ribs," Floyd said and I gaped. Did he have a sense of humor after all? Probably not. Looking at his serious expression I doubted if he had explored all the meanings of what he had just said. I let it lie.

"I'm not only unhappy with this operation so far—but with the company we have been keeping. Svinjar and his loathsome lads. We've shot almost a day here already—for little purpose. If the artifact is with the Fundamentaloids we ought to be out there tracking them down."

"But you promised a concert," Madonette pointed out with a certain logic. "They are building a sort of bandstand and the word has gone out. You don't want to let our fans down, do you?"

"Heaven forbid," I muttered gruelly and put the bowl aside. I couldn't tell them about the thirty-day poison or the fact that as of the moment over seventeen days had passed. Oh the hell with it. "Let's get set up. Maybe a quick rehearsal to see if all the gear is working and, hopefully, we are still in good form."

We put lunch aside with a great deal of pleasure and

humped our packs to the concert site. There was a grove of trees here that were serving as supports for a singularly crude platform. Planks had been set up between them, with an occasional support stuck in below if the thing sagged too much. Our audience was reluctantly and suspiciously gathering in the surrounding field. Small family units with the men all armed with swords or cudgels, keeping close watch on the womenfolk. Well, this was a slave-holding society so such concern was easily understood.

"At least they are trying to make it look nice," Madonette said, pointing. Pretty crude and crummy, I thought, but spoke not my thoughts aloud. Shuffling slaves had brought up leafy branches which they were arranging around the platform; there were even a few flowers stuck in among the leaves. Oh, things were really swinging on Liokukae tonight.

I was depressing myself sorely and did not want to pass it on to the others. "Here we go, gang!" I said swinging my pack up onto the platform and clambering behind it. "Our first live performance for this waiting world. If you don't count that quick gig upon arrival. Let's show them what a pack of real rats can do!"

With our appearance the assembling audience took heart and moved closer; latecomers hurried to their places. While we tuned up and played a riff or two, I rolled some thunder effects that had people looking at the sky. When we were ready to go, Svinjar himself came trundling through the crowd, a couple of armed heavies at his side. With their help he climbed onto the platform and raised his arms. The silence was total. Maybe it was respect, perhaps hatred and fear—or all of them rolled together. But it worked. He smiled around at the gathering, lifted his great gut so he could hook his thumbs into his belt. And spoke.

"Svinjar takes care of his people. Svinjar is your friend. Svinjar brings you The Stainless Steel Rats and their magic music. Now let us hear a big cheer for them!"

We got a big murmur which had to do. While he had been speaking his bully-boys had manhandled a sizable padded chair up onto the platform; it creaked when he dropped into it.

"Play," he ordered and sat back to enjoy the music.

"Okay, gang, ready to go!" I blew into my lapel microphone and my amplified breath gusted across the audience. "Well, hello there music lovers. By popular appeal—and the fact that we were busted by the narcs—we have come to your sunny planet to bring you the music known right around the galaxy. It is our very great pleasure now to dedicate this next song to the concert master himself, Svinjar—" He nodded acceptance and I rolled a drumroll out across the surrounding fields.

"A song that you will all know, and hopefully love, something that we can all feel, share, enjoy together, laugh together and cry together. I bring you our own and original version of that classic of modern musicality—'The Itchy Foot Itch'!"

There were shouts of joy, screams of pain, wild enthusiasm. As we launched into this overamplified and very catchy—if not itchy—number.

> *I get up at dawn and look at the river*
> *The mist rising there it gives me a shiver.*
> *Leaves on the trees they're wet with dew*
> *Looking at them I think of you—*
> *Far far away from me today*
> *I don't like it—but all I can say*
> *Is the galaxy's wide and I like to stray*
> *To the stars and beyond 'cause that's my way*
> *I got the—*
> *Itchy foot, itchy foot, itchy foot itch!*
> *Gotta keep going, never get rich!*
> *Itchy foot, itchy foot, itchy foot itch!*
> *Keeping me going, ain't that a bitch!*

*Itchy foot, itchy foot, itchy foot itch!*
*Keeping me going from place to place*
*Gotta keep going, what can I do?*
*Keep going forever—and I'll never see you.*
*Keep on going round the galaxy—no place is home*
*For the likes of mee-ee-e-e!*

There was a vast amount of itchy foot stomping, let me tell you. And plenty of cheers and cries of joy when we had finished. Buoyed up by enthusiasm we played two more numbers before I called a break.

"Thanks folks, thanks much—you're a great audience. Now if you will give us a few minutes we'll be right back . . ."

"Very well done, well done indeed," Svinjar said, waddling over and plucking the microphone from my lapel. "I know that we all have heard these musicians before—on the box—so their delightful entertainment comes as no surprise to us all. Yet still, there is something fine about having them here in person. I am grateful—I know that everyone out there is grateful." He turned and smiled broadly at me. A smile that, I could see quite clearly, held no warmth or humor at all. He turned back and spread his arms wide.

"I am so grateful that I have prepared a little surprise for all of you out there—do you want to know what it is?"

Absolute silence now—and a sideways shuffling by the audience. They apparently did not like any of Svinjar's little surprises.

They were right.

"Go!" he shouted into the microphone, so loudly that his amplified voice rolled and echoed like thunder. "Go—go—GO!"

I staggered and almost fell as the platform shook and vibrated. There was a roar of masculine voices as out from under our feet, brushing aside the disguising leafy boughs, burst a mass of armed men. More and more appeared, waving cudgels, howling as they ran, bearing down on the fleeing audience. We looked on dumbfounded as men and women were clubbed to the ground, chained, tied. The attack was brief and vicious and quickly over with. The fields were empty, the last visitor gone. Those that remained were bound and silent, or groaning with pain. Over their moans of agony Svinjar's laughter sounded clearly. He was rocking in his chair, possessed by sadistic humor, tears rolling down his cheeks.

"But where—" Madonette said. "Where did they all come from? There was no one under here when we started the concert."

I jumped to the ground, kicked some branches aside, saw the gaping mouth of the tunnel. The opening had been concealed by a dirt-covered lid, now thrown aside. There was a heavy thud and Svinjar landed beside me.

"Wonderful, isn't it?" He gestured at the opening. "I have had my men digging that thing for months now. Stamping the removed dirt into the mud whenever it rains. I had planned a meeting here, some gifts, all very vague. Until you showed up! If I were capable of gratitude I would be grateful. I am not. The blind workings of chance. And victory to those—meaning me—who have the intelligence to seize the opportunity. Now a small celebration. We will have food and drink and you will play for me."

He turned and issued instructions, kicked one of his new slaves when she stumbled close.

"It would be nice to kill him," Madonette said. Speaking for all of us, if the nodding heads meant anything.

"Caution," I cautioned. "He has all the cards and the thugs right now. Let's play the concert and figure out how we can get out of here after that."

It wasn't going to be easy. Svinjar's oversized log cabin was filled with his men. Drinking but not drunk, boasting of their feats, drinking even more. We played a number but no one was listening.

Yes; Svinjar was. Listening and looking. Waddling towards us, silencing the music with a swipe of his hand. Dropping into his chair and fingering the hilt of his large sword embedded in the stone close by his hand. Smiling that humorless smile at me again.

"Life is a bit different here, isn't it Jim?"

"You might say that."

If he was looking for trouble I wasn't going to supply it. I didn't like the odds at all.

"We make our own life—and our own rules here. Out there in the androgynous, settled worlds of the galaxy, the effete intellectuals rule. Men who act like women. Here we hearken back to the days of the primitive, virile, important men. Strength through strength. I like that. And I make the rules here." He looked at Madonette in a singularly repulsive manner.

"A fine singer—and a lovely woman," he said, then looked at me. "Your wife you say? Can anything be done about that? Let me think—yes—something can be done. Out there, in those so-called civilized planets nothing could be done. Here it can. For I am Svinjar—and Svinjar can always do something."

He lifted one gross hand and tapped me on the forehead. "By my law and my custom I now divorce you." He heaved himself to his feet while his henchmen roared with laughter at his subtle humor.

"That is not possible. It can't be done—"

For his size he was fast, whipping out the broadsword from the niche in his throne.

"Here is my first lesson for my new bride. *Nobody* says no to Svinjar."

The blade slashed out to slit my throat.

# CHAPTER 9

I jumped back to avoid the slash, stumbled over a man's legs, fell on top of him.

"Hold him!" Svinjar shouted and I was grabbed tightly, struggled to get free, couldn't quite make it.

Svinjar was standing over me, pushing the point of the sword into my throat—

Then he toppled sideways and fell with a great thud. Revealing the fact that Steengo, despite age and overweight, had jumped to the attack and was behind him, had dropped him with a chop to the neck.

What was happening had by this time sunk into even the tiniest of the birdbrains present. Men struggled to draw weapons and roared crude oaths. I saw Floyd laying about the warriors nearest him—but it wouldn't be enough. In about two seconds there was going to be a massacre of musicians if I didn't do something to stop it.

I did. First by planting my elbow in the solar plexus of my captor. Who gurgled and let go of my arms. One second gone. I didn't waste any time trying to stand up but writhed on my side and pulled the black sphere from my pocket, thumbed the actuator and threw it up towards the ceiling.

Two seconds. Weapons swinging on all sides. My best defense was to jam the filter plugs into my nostrils. The gas bomb popped and I spent a busy few seconds more dodging my attackers. Who moved more and more slowly until they dropped. When I looked around I saw that the gas had done a great job. The entire great room was filled with prone and snoring forms. I shook my hands over my head.

"Let's hear it for the good guys!" I had an audience of one, myself, which made the victory no less sweet. The sleep gas had hit my friends as well, though Floyd had been doing quite well before he dropped. A number of crumpled bodies were collapsed around him. I opened my pack and got the gas antidote, one by one I shot up my companions with the styrette. Then went to the door and stared gloomily out at the rain until they revived.

Soft footsteps behind me and Madonette held me lightly by the arms.

"Thanks, Jim."

"Was nothing."

"It was something. You saved our lives."

"We're still in it," Floyd said. "And like Madonette said, we owe you a good bit of thanks." Steengo nodded agreement.

"I wish you didn't. If this operation had been planned better all these emergencies wouldn't be taking place. My fault. I'm under what you might call a certain kind of time pressure. For reasons I can't go into right now we have to find the artifact and finish this operation within twenty days."

"That's not much time," Steengo said.

"Right—so let's not waste any of it. Our welcome has worn out around here. Grab weapons because we might have trouble getting out of town empty-handed. Packs on, armed to kill, ruthless and deadly expressions. Forward!"

After what had almost happened to us with Svinjar and his macho swinemen we were in no mood to be trifled with. It must have shown in our faces—or more likely in the metal of our weapons—because the few people we met slipped away as soon as they saw us. The rain had almost stopped and the sun was burning through and raising trails of mist from the water-logged ground. The hovels were farther apart now, the mounds of garbage fewer and more easily avoided. Straggly little bushes began to appear, then trees and larger shrubs covering the easy slope of the rolling hills. Mixed in were low bushes from which hung hard-skinned spheres the size of a man's fist. Maybe these were the polpettone trees we had been told about. This would have to be investigated—but not now. I led on at a good pace, not calling a halt until we had reached the concealment of the first coppice. I looked back at the crude buildings, with the great bulk of the Pentagon rising behind them.

"No one seems to be following us—so let's keep it that way. Five-minute break every hour, keep walking until sunset."

I touched the skull-computer hanging from my neck and the keyboard snapped into existence. I summoned up the holomap, glanced up at the sun—then pointed ahead.

"We go thataway."

It was tiring at first, struggling up one hill and down the other side, then up again. But we soon left the trees and the rolling countryside behind and marched out onto a grassy plain. We stopped for a break at the end of the first hour, dropped down and drank some water. The bravest of us chewed industriously on the concentrated rations. Which had the texture of cardboard—if not the same exciting flavor. There was a grove of the polpettone trees close by and I went and picked a few of the spherical fruits. Hard as rocks and looking just about as appetizing. I put them into my pack for later examination. Floyd had dug a small flute out of his pack and played a little jig that lifted our spirits. When we stepped out again it was to a jolly marching tune.

Madonette walked beside me, humming in time with the flute. A strong walker, she seemed to be enjoying the effort. And surely a great singer, good voice. Good everything—and that included her bod. She turned and caught me looking at

her and smiled. I looked away, slowed a bit to walk next to
Steengo for a change. He was keeping up with the rest of us
and did not look tired I was happy to see. Ahh, Madonette
. . . Think of something else, Jim, keep your eye on the job.
Not the girl. Yes, I know, she looked a lot better than anything
else around. But this was no time to go all smarmy and dewy-
eyed.

"How long you think until dark?" Steengo asked. "That
pill you gave me is wearing off with a vengeance."

I projected a holo of a watch. "I truly don't know—because I don't even know the length of the day here. This
watch, like the computer, is on ship's time. It's been a good
long time since they threw us out the gate." I squinted at the
sky. "And I don't think that sun has moved very much at all.
Time to ask for some advice."

I bit down three times hard on the left side of my jaw,
which should have triggered a signal on the jawbone radio.

*"Tremearne here."* The words bounced around clearly inside my skull.

"I read you."

"You read what?" Steengo asked.

"Please—I'm talking on the radio."

"Sorry."

*"Reception clear at this end. Report."*

"We were less than charmed by the Machmen. We left
town a couple of hours ago and are hiking out across the
plain . . ."

*"I have you on the chart, satellite location."*

"Any of the Fundamentaloid bands in sight as well?"

*"A number of them."*

"Any of them close to this position?"

*"Yes, one off to your left. Roughly the same distance you've
walked already."*

"Sounds a winner. But one important question first. How
long are the days here?"

*"About one hundred standard hours."*

"No wonder we're beginning to feel tired—and it's still full daylight. With the total daylight at least four times longer than what we're used to. Can you put your satellite to work looking back the way we came—to see if we are being followed?"

*"I've already done that. No pursuers in sight."*

"That's great news. Over and out." I raised my voice. "Company—halt. Fall out. I'll give you the other side of the conversation that you didn't hear. We're not being followed." I waited until the ragged cheer had died away. "Which means we are stopping here for food, drink, sleep, the works."

I slung my pack to the ground, stretched largely, then dropped down and leaned against it, pointed to the distant horizon. "The Fundamentaloid nomads are somewhere out in that direction. We are going to have to find them sooner or later—and I vote for later."

"Vote seconded, motion passed." They were all horizontal now. I took a good swig of water before I went on.

"The days here are four times as long as the ones that we are used to. I think that we have had enough of fighting, walking, everything for one day, or a quarter of a day, or whatever. Let's sleep on it and go on when we are rested."

My advice was unneeded since eyelids were already closing. I could do no less myself and was drifting off when I realized this was not the world's greatest idea. I heaved myself, groaning, to my feet and walked away from the others so my voice would not disturb them.

"Come in Tremearne. Can you read me."

*"Sergeant Naenda here. The Captain is off duty this watch. Should I send for him?"*

"Not if you are sitting in for him—and you have the satellite observations handy and up-to-date."

*"Affirmative."*

"Well keep looking at them. We're taking a sleep break

now and I would like it to be undisturbed. If you see anyone or anything creeping up on us—give a shout."

*"Will do. Nighty-night."*

Nighty-night! What were the armed forces coming to? I stumbled back to my companions and emulated their fine example. I had no trouble at all in falling asleep.

It was waking up that was difficult. Some hours had slipped by because when I blinked blearily up at the sky I saw that the sun had passed the meridian and was finally slipping down towards the horizon. What had wakened me?

*"Attention, Jim diGriz, attention."*

I looked around for the speaker and it took long seconds before I realized that it was Captain Tremearne's voice I was hearing.

"Wazza?" I said incoherently, still numbed with sleep.

*"One of the Fundamentaloid bands is on the move—roughly in your direction. They should be close enough to see you in about an hour."*

"By which time we should be ready for visitors. Thanks, Cap—over and out."

My stomach snarled at me and I realized that the concentrated rations had been a little too concentrated. I drank some water to wash the taste of sleep from my mouth, then poked Floyd with my toe. His eyes snapped open and I smiled sweetly.

"You have just volunteered to go to those bushes over there and get some firewood. It is breakfast time."

"Right, breakfast, wood, wonderful." He climbed to his feet, yawned and stretched, scratched at his beard then went off on his mission. I gathered up enough dry grass to make a small pile, then dug the atomic battery out of my pack. It would power our musical equipment for at least a year, so it could spare a few volts now. I pulled the insulation off the ends of the wires on a short lead, shorted them to produce a fat snap of sparks, pushed it into the grass. In a moment the grass was burning nicely, crackling and smoking, and ready for the chunks of dry branches that Floyd brought back. When it was good and hot I dropped the polpettone into the glowing ashes.

The rest of the band stirred in their sleep when the smoke blew their way, but didn't really wake up until I broke one of the fruits open. The skin was black so I hoped it was done. The rich seasoned fragrance of cooked meat wafted out and everyone was awake in an instant.

"Yum," I said, chewing on a fragrant morsel. "My thanks to the genetic engineers who dreamed this one up. Gourmet food—and growing on trees. If it weren't for the inhabitants this planet would be a paradise."

After we had dined and were feeling relatively human I made my report to them.

"I've been in touch with the eye in the sky. A band of nomads is coming this way. I figured that we should let them do the walking instead of us. Are we now prepared for contact?"

There were quick nods and no hesitant looks I was happy to see. Steengo hefted his ax and glowered. "Ready as we'll ever be. I just hope this lot is a bit more friendly than the first bunch."

"Only one way to find out." I bit down three times hard. "Where are the Fundamentaloids now?"

*"Crossing a bit north of you—beyond those shrubs on the slight rise."*

"Then here we go. Packs on, weapons ready, fingers crossed. Forward!"

We walked slowly up the hill and through the shrubs—and stopped in our tracks and stared at the herd passing slowly by.

"Sheots," I said. "The mutant cross between sheep and goats that they told us about."

"Sheots," Madonette agreed. "But they didn't tell us they were so huge! I don't even come up to their legpits."

"Indeed," I agreed. "Something else about them. They're big enough to ride upon. And if I am not mistaken we have been seen and those three riders are galloping our way."

"And waving weapons," Steengo said grimly. "Here we go again."

# CHAPTER 10

They thundered towards us, swords waving, sharp black hooves kicking up clouds of dust. The sheots had nasty little eyes, wicked, curved horns—and what looked very much like tusks. I couldn't recall ever seeing a sheep or a goat with tusks, but there is always a first time.

"Stay in line, weapons ready," I called out, swinging my own sword up. The nearest rider, draped in black, pulled hard on the reins and his woolly mount skidded to a stop. He frowned down on me from behind his great black beard, spoke in a deep and impressive voice.

"Those who live by the sword shall die by the sword. So it is written."

"You talking about yourself?" I queried, blade still ready.

"We are men of peace, infidel, but defend our flocks against numberless rustlers."

He could be telling the truth; I had to take the chance. I plunged my sword into the dirt and stepped back. But was ready to grab it in an instant.

"We are men of peace as well. But go armed for our own protection in this wicked world."

He thought about that for a bit, made the decision. He slipped the sword into a leather scabbard, then swung down from his mount. The beast instantly opened its mouth—and those *were* tusks—and tried to bite him. He scarcely noted this, merely balled a fist and got the thing under the jaw with a swift uppercut. Its mouth clacked shut and its eyes crossed for an instant. It wasn't too long on brains either, because when its eyes uncrossed it had completely forgotten about him. It said *baa* loudly and began to graze. The rider walked over and stood before me.

"I am Arroz conPollo and these are my followers. Have you been saved?"

"I am Jim diGriz and this is my band. And I don't believe in banks."

"What are banks?"

"Where you save money. Fedha."

"You misunderstand my meaning, Jim of diGriz. It is your soul that needs saving—not your fedha."

"An interesting theological point, Arroz of conPollo. We must discuss it in some depth. What do you say we all put the weapons down and have a good chinwag. Put them away," I called out.

Arroz signaled his two companions and we all felt a lot better as the swords were sheathed, axes lowered. For the first time he looked away from me to my followers. And gasped, turned pale under his tan, and held his arm before his eyes.

"Unclean," he moaned, "unclean."

"Well it is a little hard to have a bath when you're on the trail," I told him. I didn't add that he wasn't that spic and span himself.

"Not of the body—of the spirit. Is that not a vessel of corruption among you?"

"Could you spell that out a little more clearly?"

"Is that . . . person a . . . *woman?*" He still had his arm across his face.

"The last time I looked she was." I moved sideways a bit, closer to my sword. "What's it to you?"

"Her face must be covered to conceal impurity, her ankles covered lest they promote lust in the hearts of men."

"This guy is a bit of a weirdo," Madonette said disgustedly. He yiped.

"And her voice silenced lest it lure the blessed into sin!"

Steengo nodded to Floyd and took the angry girl by the arm, but she shrugged him off. "Jim," he said. "The bunch of us are going to stroll back among the trees and have a break. See if you can sort this out."

"Right." I watched them leave and when they were out of sight looked back at the three nomads who were emulating their leader, all with their arms raised, as though sniffing their armpits. "It's safe now. Can we talk about this?"

"Return," Arroz said to his mates. "I will explain the Law to this stranger. Let the flock graze."

They trotted off while his own mount chomped away on the grass. He sat down cross-legged and motioned to me. "Sit. We must talk."

I sat. But upwind of him because it had been a long time since he or his clothes had been near soap and water. And he talked about unclean! He rooted about under his robe, had a good scratch, then withdrew a book and held it up.

"This book is the font of all wisdom," he intoned, eyes gleaming.

"That's nice. What is it called?"

"The Book. There are no other books. All that men need to know is in here. The distillate of all wisdom." I thought that it looked pretty thin for that job, but wisely kept my mouth shut. "It was the great Founder, whose name may not be spoken, who had the inspiration to read all of the Holy books of all of the ages, who saw in them the work of the god whose name may not be spoken, saw which passages were inspired and which were untrue. From all the books He distilled the true Book—then burned all of the others. He went forth into the world and His followers were many. But others were jealous and tried to destroy Him and His followers. That has been told. And it is told that to avoid this senseless persecution He and His followers came to this world where they could worship untroubled. That is why I asked—are you unclean? Or do you also follow the Way of the Book?"

"Most interesting. I follow a slightly different way. But my way believes in respecting your way, so don't worry too much about me."

He frowned at this and shook an admonitory finger at me. "There is only one Way, only one Book. All who think differently are damned. Now is your chance to be cleansed for I have shown you the true Way."

"Thanks a lot—but no thanks."

He stood up and stabbed an accusatory finger in my direction. "Unclean! Profane! Leave—for you soil me with your presence."

"Well each to their own opinion. Good-by and good luck with your sheot shearing. May all your fleeces be giant ones. But an indulgence please—before you go would you take a look at this." I pulled the photograph of the alien artifact from my pocket and held it out.

"Unclean," he muttered and put his hand behind his back so he wouldn't touch it.

"I'm sure it is. I just want to know if you have seen this thing in the picture before."

"No, never."

"Been nice talking to you."

He did not return my friendly wave as he walked over to his mount, kicked it in the leg until it sat down, climbed aboard and galloped off. I pulled my sword out of the ground and went to join the others. Madonette was still simmering.

"Hypocritical narrowminded bigoted moron."

"That and a lot more. At least I got one bit of negative information from him. He never saw the artifact. It must have been taken by another one of the tribes."

"Are we going to have to talk to all of them?"

"Unless you have any better ideas. And nineteen days to go."

"I don't trust him," Madonette said. "And don't sneer and say female intuition. Aren't these the same kind as the bunch that attacked the archeologists' ship?"

"You're right—and isn't that the clatter of hundreds of hooves coming this way?"

"It is!" Floyd shouted, pointing. "What do we do—run?"

"No! Out of the trees and onto the plain. Instruments at the ready. We are going to give these guys a concert that they will never forget!"

Arroz had gone back to rally the troops and at least thirty of them, with plenty of sword waving and maniac baaing, came charging down. I turned the amplification on the sound up until it would not go any higher.

"Earplugs in, get ready, on the count of three we give them old number thirteen, 'The Rockets Go Rumbling On.' One; two . . ."

On the count of three the explosion of unbearable sound blasted out. The lead riders were tossed to the ground as the sheots recoiled in fear. I flipped some smoke bombs among them, just to keep the action going, and hit them with holographed lightning volts.

It was pretty good. Before we got to the second chorus the stampede was over, the last terrorized sheots galloped away out of sight. The last black-robed Fundamentaloid crawled over the horizon, the trampled grass dotted with discarded swords, gobbets of fleece and myriad eightballs of dung.

"Victory is ours!" I whooped happily.

And only nineteen days to go I thought depressedly. This just would not do. I had the awful feeling that we could spend nineteen days or nineteen weeks stumbling about this planet and be no wiser about the alien artifact we were seeking.

There had to be a change of plan—and now! I walked away from the others, then bit down three times, so hard that I almost cracked a tooth.

"*Captain Tremearne here.*"

"And dismal Jim diGriz on this end. Have you been following all this?"

"*Yes, and watching. I heard you ask him to identify the photograph. I assume that he did not.*"

"You assume right, distant and disembodied voice. Now listen, there has got to be a change of plan. When I came up with the idea for this present operation I assumed that there was some kind of imitation of civilization on this dismal world. Where we could stroll from gig to gig and do our snooping at the same time. I was wrong."

"*I regret that all the facts were not supplied to you at the time. But as you are now aware there is a complete ban on information being circulated about this particular planet.*"

"I know that now—and it won't wash. We would have been a lot better if we came here disguised as a squad of combat marines. So far every bunch we have met has tried to kill us. The whole thing is that hardnosed Admiral Benbow's fault. He lied to me about what we would find here. Right?"

"*As a serving military officer I cannot discuss the conduct of my superiors. But I can agree that whoever briefed you was, I must say, economical with the truth.*"

"Do you also know that he was economical with my health? And that in nineteen days I am going to keel over from time-released poison."

"*Regrettably, I have been informed that that is the case. And you have eighteen days left now. You appear to have lost track of one day during the past period.*"

"Eighteen? Thanks much. That only makes what I have to say even more imperative. I need some help, some transportation."

*"All contact with the planet is forbidden."*

"I just changed the rules. You yourself told me that you are heading a committee to bring about major improvements here. The first change will be to get one of the ship's launches down here. With that I can get around to the various bands of sheot shaggers before my personal deadline runs out."

*"If I do that I will be disobeying orders and it could end my career."*

"Well?"

The silence inside my head went on and on. I waited. Until I heard what could only have been a sigh.

*"I suppose there are plenty of job opportunities for skilled civilians these days. The launch will land after dark. If it is not seen by anyone on the ground there is just a chance that my career change can be postponed."*

"You're a good guy, Tremearne. My heartiest thanks."

I hummed a bar or two from "The Swedish Monster" as I walked back to inform my companions.

"Jim, you're wonderful!" Madonette said, grabbed and kissed me. "I much prefer flying to walking."

Floyd nodded happy agreement and reached for me.

"Away!" I shouted. "Girls, okay, but I don't kiss guys with beards. What we do now is put a little distance between us and those religious nuts in case they want to come back for seconds. Then rest up until dark. I have a feeling that it is going to be a very busy night."

# CHAPTER 11

"Wake up, Jim—it's almost dark."

Madonette's gentle hand was most welcome, since it drew me up out of a really repulsive nightmare. Tentacles, bulging eyeballs, yukk. The eighteen-day dead deadline must be getting to my subconscious. I sat up, yawned and stretched. With great reluctance the sun had finally dropped behind the horizon leaving behind a slowly fading band of light. The stars were coming out revealing some pretty boring constellations—and very few of them at that. This prison planet must be far out on the galactic rim.

Then something blotted out the stars in the zenith as a dark form drifted down to the ground, silently on null-grav drive. The door opened as we approached—and the cabin lights came on.

"Turn them off, lunkhead!" I shouted. "You want to ruin my night vision." The pilot turned about in his seat and I grinned insincerely. "Sorry Captain, sir—that lunkhead, just a figure of speech."

"My fault completely," he said, and tapped one of his electronic eyeballs. "With these I forget. I'm piloting this thing because I have the best night vision in the fleet."

He flipped the lights off and we groped our way aboard with just the dim red emergency lights to show us the way. I sat in the copilot's seat and strapped in.

"What is your plan?" he asked.

"A simple one. You know the position of all the sheot flocks don't you?"

"Observed and logged into the launch's memory."

"Great. Have the computer do a topological survey to plot a course that will let us visit them all in the shortest amount of time. We drift over to the first flock, find one of the shepherds who is maybe out of sight of the others—and talk to him. Show him the photograph and find out if he has seen the thing. If he hasn't—on to the next bunch."

"Seems a simple and practical plan. Belts fastened? Right, first flock coming up."

We were slammed back into our seats and were on our way. High and fast on the plotted track. Then slow and drifting in low while Tremearne peered out into the darkness.

"There's one," he said. "On the far side of the flock—all by himself. Either to guard the beasts or keep them from wandering. I have a suggestion. I approach him from behind and immobilize him. Then you question him."

"Creep up in the dark? Immobilize an armed and watchful guard? That's a job for a combat trooper."

"Well how do you think I got these electronic eyeballs? It will be entertaining to do a bit of work again."

I had no choice but to agree. The Captain was proving to be an excellent ally. Working this way would be certainly a lot faster than me crawling around on my own. If he could do as he said. I had my doubts but kept them to myself. He was a gray-haired desk jockey with electric eyesight who might very well be past his sell-by date.

He wasn't. After we landed he stepped out the door and vanished silently in the darkness. Not thirty seconds later he called to me quietly.

"Over here. You can use your light now."

I turned on the handlight, it was really black under the almost starless sky, and saw two forms standing close together.

The light revealed a bulging-eyed shepherd seized in an unbreakable grip, a hand on his throat keeping him silent. I waggled the light under his nose.

"Listen, oh shepherd who failed his duty. The hand that holds you could just as easily have killed you. Then we could rustle all your woolly flock and eat sheot shashlik until the end of time. But I will be merciful. The hand will be removed from your filthy throat and you will not shout or you really will be dead. You will speak to me softly and answer my questions. You may now speak."

He coughed and groaned when the pressure was released. "Demons in the darkness! Release me, do not kill me, tell me what you wish of me then go back to the pit from which you have escaped . . ."

I reached out and tweaked his nose sharply. "Shut up. Open your eyes. Look at this photograph. Let me know if you have ever seen it before."

I held the photo close, shone the light on it. Tremearne gave a twitch of emphasis to his arm and the captive moaned his answer. "Never, no, such a thing I would remember, no—" His voice gurgled into silence and he dropped unconscious to the ground.

"Don't these sheot shepherds ever wash?" Tremearne asked.

"Only on alternate years. Let's get to the next one."

We quickly worked out a routine. We would land and he would be away. Usually, by the time I had exited the launch, he would be calling me. Many a terrified shepherd slept soundly this night. But only after looking at the picture of the artifact. I dozed between visits and the back of the launch echoed with snores and heavy breathing. Only the Captain was unsleeping and tireless, seemingly as fit on the eleventh visit as he had been on the first. It was a long, long night.

I was getting groggy by the time we hit thirteen. Unlucky

thirteen; get it over with and on to fourteen. Another set of bulging eyes peeking over the top of another matted beard. "Look!" I snarled. "Speak! And moaning does not count as speaking. Ever seen this thing?" This one gurgled instead of moaning, then yiped as his arm got twisted a bit further. It looked as though even the stolid Captain was beginning to lose his patience.

"Imp of Satan . . . work of the devil . . . I warned them, but they wouldn't listen . . . the grave, the grave!"

"Do you have any idea of what he is babbling about?" Tremearne asked.

"There may be hope, Captain. If he is not bonkers he might have seen it. Look—see! Ever see before?"

"I told him not touch it—death and damnation were sure to follow."

"You have seen it. All right, Cap, you can let up on the arm—but stand ready." I rooted in my pocket and took out a handful of silver cylinders, the local money, let the light shine on them. "Hey you, Smelly, look—fedha—and all for you. All yours."

This got his attention all right and I closed my fist tight as he groped for them. "Yours if you answer some simple questions. You will not be hurt—but only if you answer truthfully. You have seen this thing?"

"They fled. We found it in their skyship. I touched it, unclean, unclean."

"You're doing fine." I shook half of the coins into his waiting hand. "Now the ten-thousand-fedha question. Where is it now?"

"Sold, sold to them. The Paradisians. May they be cursed by it, cursed forever . . ."

It wasn't easy, but we finally worked all the details out of him. Stripped of all the curses and blasphemy it was a simple tale of larceny and chicanery. The spacer had landed—and been attacked as soon as the door had been opened. During the fracas the Fundamentaloids had trundled through the ship and grabbed everything portable, including the container with the alien artifact. They had carried the whole thing away with them because they had a job opening it. When they eventually succeeded they could not understand what it was. And ignorance meant fear. So they had unloaded it in the market in Paradise where almost anything could be sold. End of story.

We let the shepherd keep the money when we lowered him, unconscious, to the ground. "This calls for consultation," I said.

"Yes, but not this close to the flock. Let's get up to the plateau where the air is fresher."

The others were awake when we landed this time, listening closely to what we had discovered.

"Well this narrows the field a bit," Madonette said.

"Does it?" I asked. "How big is the population of this paradisaical nation?"

"Around one hundred thousand," Tremearne admitted. "It may not be the best society on this planet but it appears to be the most successful one. I know very little about it, just photographs and observation."

"Doesn't anyone in the Pentagon know more?"

"Probably. But the information is classified and they aren't talking."

I cracked my knuckles, scowled and jabbed my finger at him. "That's really not good enough—is it?"

Tremearne looked as unhappy as I did. "No, Jim, it is not. I don't know why all that information is classified while your group is actually operating here on the planet. I have tried to get the information and have been not only rebuffed but warned off."

"Who is doing this? Any idea?"

"None—other than that it is at the very highest level. The people I have been in contact with understand your problems and want to help. But any requests that they pass on are turned down instantly and with prejudice."

"Am I paranoid—or is there someone in the chain of command who doesn't like this operation? Who wants it to fail?"

It was Tremearne's turn now to crack his knuckles and look glum.

"I've told you—I am a career officer. But I'm not fond of the situation here on this planet. Not only the way your group is being treated, but the whole ugly business. Well, I feel that it is getting away from me. At first I thought I could get some reform here by working through channels. It's not good enough. I am being blocked just as completely as you are."

"Who—and why?"

"I don't know. But I am doing my best to find out. About this city and the Paradisians I guess, basically, I know absolutely nothing."

"An honest answer, Captain, and I thank you for it."

"If you don't know—why then we'll just have to find out for ourselves," Steengo said. "Play a gig or two and keep our eyes open."

"May it be so easy," I muttered under my breath. "Roll out the maps."

It looked as though the largest part of the population was located in the single straggling city. Roads led from it to not-too-distant villages and there were scatterings of other buildings that might be farms. The only really puzzling thing about the 3D map was what looked like a wall that appeared to cut the city in two. There were no walls around the city, just this single one in the middle. I pointed to it.

"Any idea what this is—or what it means?"

Tremearne shook his head. "No idea. Looks like a wall,

that's all. But there is a road alongside it. Which appears to be the only road leading in from the plain."

I poked my finger into the holomap.

"Here. Where the road fades and runs out in the grass. That's where we have to go. Unless anyone has a better idea?"

"Looks good to me," Tremearne said. "I'll land you on this bit of plateau, beyond this ridge where we won't be seen. Then I'll take the launch out of there and stay in touch with you by radio."

We unloaded. "Sleep first," Floyd yawned. "It's been a long night."

It was even longer than that, what with the longer days here. Tremearne took off and we settled down to sleep. We slept, and woke up and it was still dark. Slept some more. At least the others snored on: I had too much on my mind to drift off as easily as they did. We had a clue now to the whereabouts of the alien artifact. A clue that was useless until we started looking. And we couldn't look in the darkness. And I had— how many days left before the thirty-day poison zonked me? I counted on my fingers. Just about eighteen gone, which left twelve to go. Wonderful. Or had I counted wrong? I started again with the fingers, then grew angry with myself. Enough with the fingers already. I clicked on my computer and wrote a quick program. Then touched $D$ for deadline—or death, whatever—and a glowing eighteen appeared before me accompanied by a flickering twelve. Not that I enjoyed looking at them, mind you, but this way I could stop worrying about the changing count. Some part of me must have been satisfied with this because I fell deeply asleep.

Finally, with great reluctance and sloth, the sky lightened and another day began. Before it was completely light the Captain drifted the launch in low and slow behind the hills, boarded us, then let us out behind the final ridge.

"Good luck," he said, with a certain grimness. The port

ground shut and the launch moved away and vanished in the growing light. Scarcely aware of what I was doing I punched *D* into the computer. The numbers snapped into existence, vanished just as quickly. But I remembered.

Day nineteen.

# CHAPTER 12

Dawn crept on interminably as we walked, the sun dragging itself up over the horizon only with great reluctance. It was still not quite full daylight when we came to what had to be the beginning of the wall. Just a single row of bricks almost hidden in the grass.

"What do you think?" I asked of no one in particular. Steengo bent and rapped one with his knuckles.

"Brick," he said.

"Red brick," Madonette said brightly.

"Thanks, thanks," I mumbled with complete lack of appreciation.

There was a barely visible path next to the right-hand side of the row of bricks; for want of a better idea we began walking along it.

"It's higher, see," Floyd said, pointing. "A second course has been added."

"And more still ahead," Madonette said. "Three bricks high now."

"What's this?" Steengo said, bending and pushing the grass aside to look more closely, touching the brick with his fingertip. "There's some kind of symbol stamped into each of the bricks." We all looked now.

"Sort of a circle with an arrow sticking out of it."

"Arrow . . . circle," I muttered. A sudden intuition bounced about inside my skull. "I've seen that symbol before —yes indeed! Would someone kindly step over the wall and see if there is a circle with a cross sticking out of it on the other side."

Madonette lifted lovely eyebrows with curiosity, stepped daintily over the low wall, bent and looked. Eyebrows even higher now.

"How did you do that? On this side there is a circle-cross sign stamped into each brick."

"Biology," I said. "I remembered from school."

"Yes, of course," she said, stepping back. "The symbols for male and female."

Floyd had strolled on ahead; he called out. "Right as rain. Here is *VIROJ* stamped into a brick. And," he leaned over and looked, "*VIRINOJ* on the other side."

Very gradually the wall became higher as we walked beside it. In addition to the symbols we came to *LJUDI* then *MTUWA*, *HERRER, SIGNORI*.

"Enough," I said, stopping. "Packs off. We shall now take our break while we see what we have here. The message seems to be clear enough. Look at the path we have been following. Is there another path on the other side as well?"

The brick wall was as high as our waists now; Floyd put one hand on it and vaulted over, bent and looked.

"Maybe, but not too clear. Could have been here once but it is so overgrown with grass that it is hard to tell. Can I come back now?"

"Yes—because it's about time for a decision." I pointed ahead to the slowly heightening wall. "The Fundamentaloids said they came to the city to trade. So they must have come this way, possibly made this track that we are following."

Madonette nodded agreement—and didn't like it. "And they were all men, I remember that all too clearly. Unclean indeed! No women allowed. Or if the women did come this way they would have to have walked over on the other side of the wall. What do you want us to do, Jim?"

"What do *we* want to do? As I said—it's time for a decision. Do we all stick together and ignore the obvious instructions? That's the first question that we have to answer."

"Do that and I'll bet that eventually we get into some kind of trouble," she said. "A lot of serious work went into this wall. So if we don't read the message something not too nice is guaranteed to happen. It always does on this world. The choice is mine. I'll cross over and trot down the other side—"

"No," I broke in. "As we go along the wall gets higher and we'll be separated, out of contact. That won't do."

"Well I'm not staying here—and I can't go back. So we need contact, what you just said. Kindly clack your jaw-a-phone and get onto Tremearne. Tell him to get some radios down here that we can use to keep in touch. If we are going to complete this assignment the right way, we will have to know what is going on on both sides of the wall. And I'm the only one who can find out what happens—here."

She picked up her pack and planted her bottom on the wall, swung her legs up and over and smiled at us from the other side. I didn't like it.

"It's not a matter of liking or not liking it," she said reading my doubts from my expression. "It is just the only way that we can get the job done. Get the radios. Don't forget that Tremearne will always be listening in and can send the marines if any of us gets into trouble. Call him."

"I will. But let us make sure they are the right kind of radios before we put in the order. Line of sight is going to be out with the wall standing in the way and blocking the signal. Plus—who knows how thick the thing is going to be? It could soak up all the radio frequencies and that would be the end of that. Anyone know of a kind of radio that shoots a signal through rocks?"

I was speaking my thoughts aloud, half in jest. So was more than a little surprised when a voice behind me said, "Yes."

I spun about and glared at Steengo who was buffing his fingernails on his shirt, then admiring his image in their shining surfaces.

"You said that?" I accused. He nodded sagely. "Why?"

"*Why* is a good question. The answer is that although I stand before you, an aging amateur musician drawn from retirement to risk his life for the public good, it should not be forgotten that I worked for many a decade in the cause of that same public good. League communications. Where I helped develop a neat little device referred to as MIPSC."

"Mipsic?" I echoed inanely.

"Close enough, my good friend Jim. MIPSC is the acronym of Miniaturized Personal Satellite Communicator. I suggest that you clamp your jaw and order up a brace of them. Although four would be better—that way we could all keep in touch at all times. And remind Tremearne to put a commsatellite into orbit as well. Geostationary over the city of Paradise."

"*MIPSCs are not only highly secret but incredibly expensive,*" Tremearne said when I contacted him.

"Just like this little task force. Can you do it?"

"*Of course. They're on the way.*"

A half an hour later a small package drifted down from the sky hanging from a grav-lifter—which zipped up and vanished as soon as the package had been removed. I popped the end open and shook out a handful of false fingernails. I popped my eyes at these—then remembered how Steengo had been buffing his own fingernails when he told me about MIPSC.

"Tricky," I said.

"High tech and perfect concealment," he said. "There should be glue in the package. They come in pairs. The one marked *E* goes onto the index finger, left hand. *M* glued to the pinkie of the same hand. Inside the nails are holographed circuitry so they can be trimmed as small as needed to fit. Without damaging the circuits in any way."

"*E? M?*" Floyd asked.

"Earplugs and microphone."

"Then what?" I asked, almost humbly, dazed by the sudden appearance of a communications wizard in our midst.

"They are powered by the destruction of the phagocytes that come to eat them where they touch the cuticle. Which means that the power is always on. Anytime you are outside—or in a building with thin floors—your signal zips up to the satellite and back down to the other receiver. Simple. Just put your index finger into your ear and talk into the microphone on your pinkie."

I measured a pair, trimmed and glued with, I must admit, a certain amount of trepidation. Stuck my finger into my ear and said, "I hope it works."

*"Of course it does,"* Tremearne said, speaking through my fingernail instead of my jaw for a change.

While we had been installing the MIPSCs we had been going over and over all of the possibilities, had returned always to the only viable plan.

"Let's do it," Madonette said, admiring her new communicating fingernails. She put on her pack, shrugged it into comfortable position, then turned and walked off on her side of the barrier. With each step the wall grew higher, until, very quickly, it was as high as her head, then higher. After a last wave of her hand she vanished from sight.

"Keep in touch," I said into my pinkie. "Regular reports and sing out if you see anything—anything at all."

*"Just as you say, boss."*

We slipped on our packs and started walking. By the time an hour had passed the wall was high and unscalable. Though I stayed in radio contact with her, Madonette was now completely alone. I kept telling myself that armed help could zip down from the orbiting spacer if needed. This did not make me feel much better.

"First tilled fields coming up," Floyd said. "And more

than that. That dust cloud next to the wall—it's coming our way."

"Weapons ready—and I have some concussion grenades handy if things get hairy."

We stopped and waited and watched. In the distance it looked like a horse that was trotting towards us.

"Horse—but no rider," I said.

Steengo had the keener vision. "Looks like no horse I ever saw before. Not one with six legs."

It slowed to a stop and looked at us. We returned the favor. A robot, metal. Jointed legs and in the front a pair of tentacle-like arms to boot. No head to speak of, just a couple of eyes that rose up on a stalk. A loudspeaker between its arms rustled and squawked metallically.

"*Bonan tagon—kaj bonvenu al Paradizo.*"

"And a good day to you as well," I said. "My name is Jim."

"A masculine surname, most agreeable. I am called Hingst and it is my pleasure to greet you—"

The creature's words were drowned out by a throbbing roar and a cloud of black smoke emerged from its rear. We stepped back, weapons ready. Hingst's flexible arms lifted straight up.

"I wish you only peace, oh strangers. You would not know it, since you are untutored in science, but the sound and fumes are merely the exhaust of my alcohol engine. Which is rapidly turning a generator which in turn . . ."

"Charges up your batteries. We know a thing or two as well, Hingst, greeter of strangers to Paradise, and we are not your usual goaty nomads."

"Now that *is* a pleasure to hear, visiting gentlemen. Before my operating system was bolted into this rather crude construction I was a class A42 headwaiterbot and worked at only the most excellent restaurants . . ."

"Another time," I said. "I would enjoy your reminiscences. We have a few questions—"

"And I am sure I have a few answers," it said with surly overtones. "But there are preliminaries to go through." It had strolled a few paces forward as it talked and now, like a striking snake, one of its tentacles lashed at me. I jumped back, lifted my sword—but not before the cool metal tip had touched my lips and just as swiftly been withdrawn.

"Try that again and you'll be a tentacle short," I growled.

"Temper, temper. After all you are armed strangers and I am simply doing my duty. Which is to sample your saliva. And test it, which I have done. You may proceed, Gentleman Jim, because you indeed are of the male sex. I would appreciate samples from your associates."

"As long as it is just spit you are after," Floyd growled, hands joined and cupped over his nether regions.

"Oh, I do appreciate a sense of humor, stranger." The tentacle took its sample from his mouth. "Gentleman stranger I can now say. Final traveler if you please. Lovely, thank you. You may now proceed."

It turned away and I jumped in front of it.

"A moment first, Hingst the Official Greeter. A few questions . . ."

"Sorry. I am not programmed for that. Kindly step aside, Gentleman Jim."

"Only after I get a few answers."

When I didn't move the other tentacle touched my arm— and lightning struck!

I was lying dizzily on the ground watching it trot away. "Shocking, isn't it!" Hingst called back smugly. "*Big* batteries."

Floyd helped me to my feet and dusted me off. "So good so far."

"Thanks. But you aren't the one who was short-circuited."

I reported to Madonette as we went on, with Tremearne

listening in. *"Applied technology,"* he said. *"Perhaps this lot isn't as bad as the rest of the crumb-bums on this planet."* Since I was still tingling, and had a burnt taste in my mouth, I sneered in silence and did not bother to answer. Very soon after that Madonette called in that a creature like the one we had described was coming towards her. I clutched my sword in helpless anger, relaxed only when she called back.

*"Just like you—only with a different name. Hoppe. As soon as it made the test it trotted off. What now?"*

"We go on—and you take a break. If things are going to be the same, or similar, on both sides of the wall we'll find out first."

*"Male chauv superiority?"*

"Common sense. We're three to your one."

*"A solid argument—and I could use the rest. Keep in contact."*

"You've got it. Here we go."

The path had widened and was more of a dirt road now. We passed some tilled fields and came to a large grove of polpettone trees. Obviously cultivated since they were planted in neat rows. Beyond them was a low huddle of buildings that could be a farm.

Blocking the path was a brick building with an archway that spanned the road; we slowed and stopped.

"Is that what I think it is?" Steengo said.

"I think that it is a building with an arch under it," Floyd said. "And we're not going to find out any more just standing around here."

We shuffled forward slowly and stopped again when a man appeared in the archway. Our hands twitched away from our weapons when he stepped out into the sunlight. He blinked his red-rimmed eyes against the glare, nodded his head so his mane of long white hair bobbed, then tapped the arrow-and-circle symbol picked out in white on the front of his gray robe.

"Welcome, strangers, welcome to Paradise. I am Afatt, the

official greeter. Market opens at dawn tomorrow. You may stay out here, or if you wish to camp beyond the arch your weapons will be looked after until you return. A payment of one fedha is required for attendance."

The way he flicked a look over his shoulder as he said this strongly suggested that what he wanted was more bribe than payment.

"No way, aged Afatt," I intoned. "Those you see before you are not peasant traders but galaxy-famous chart-topping musicians. We are . . . *The Stainless Steel Rats!*"

His jaw dropped and he stepped back a pace. "Don't need no rats in Paradise. A rusty, chipped old fedha will do . . ."

"We got a real fan in old Afatt here," Floyd muttered. "I thought the planet was hip-deep in TV sets?"

A more military Paradisian appeared in the archway. Younger, bigger, and he came complete with studded metal helmet and heavy leather trappings. "What did you say?" he said as he swung a shining and singularly nasty looking ax.

"You heard me, Sunny. I don't repeat myself for the troops."

This provoked a twisted snarl and a barked command.

"Guard—fall out. We got some sheot shaggers here that need a lesson in civility."

This was followed instantly by the clanking of metal and the thud of running feet.

Many of them.

# CHAPTER 13

There were a lot of them, armed with a collection of nasty and lethal-looking weapons. I must learn to control impetuosity in speech on this slumworld. Think quickly, Jim, before things get any worse.

"I tempted a jest, good sir. I will be happy to repeat myself for your benefit. You, and your good men, have the pleasure of being in the presence of the finest musicians in the known galaxy!"

As I spoke I touched the remote control on the side of my backpack and a mighty organ sounded out the opening bars of "Mutants of Mercury." Floyd and Steengo quickly joined in with the opening lines.

> One head good—but two heads better—
> Got brown eyes like an English setter . . .

The effect of this little jingle of genetic jest was very impressive. As a man the soldiers roared aloud and surged towards us.

"Do we fight or run?" Floyd said grimly, grabbing at his sword.

I started to shout *fight*—but at the last instant called out—"Listen!"

For they had forgotten about their weapons and were shouting with joy!

"It's them, like on the Galactic Greasecutter show . . ."

"The hairy, ugly one—that's Floyd!"

"I want to hear 'How Much Is the Snakey in the Snakepit'!"

Then they were around us, trying to shake our hands and emitting hoarse cries of fannish enthusiasm.

"But—but—" I but-butted. "Your official greeter never heard of us?"

The first soldier, snarls now turned to smiles, not too gently pushed the old man aside. "Afatt never looks at the boggle gox. But we do! Let me tell you it was like suicidesville around here when we heard that you were sent down. Should have known that you would have to end up here. Wait until the boys in the barracks hear about this. There'll be a crackup in the old kaserne tonight!"

They escorted us cheerily under the arch and onto the drillfield beyond, our new host proudly leading the way.

"I'm Ljotur, Sergeant of the Guard. You all take it easy while I call this in. Drinks!" he ordered his men. "And food—whatever they want."

This was more like it. The beer tasted like beer, although it was of an interesting green color. The soldiers crowded close, hanging on every word we said, so I chomped my jaw to get Tremearne's attention and made my report to him in the form of a speech.

"Gallant warriors of Paradise—we are overwhelmed by your greeting. You have welcomed we drug-ridden convicts as heroes to your fair land. You ply us with food and drink and, by your loud cheers, I feel we have a beautiful future here."

"*I certainly hope so,*" Tremearne's voice said inside my head. "*But until you find out the score on this male-female thing I am ordering Madonette to stay where she is.*"

"I agree completely," I called out. "Don't you agree completely, guys, that this is the warmest welcome we have ever received?"

My companions nodded without interrupting the flow of food and drink and there were gurgled shouts of agreement from all sides as more beer vanished. I was wiping my lips with the back of my hand when Ljotur reappeared.

"I have talked to Iron John himself who summons you to his presence soonest. But until the Chariots of Fire appear could you—oh, would you!—play us a number!"

His words were drowned out by hearty masculine cries of joy.

"Let's set up for a quick gig, boys—these guys deserve it." I looked around. "Any requests?"

Many were shouted, but "Nothing's Too Bad For the Enemy" seemed to be most popular. Best choice too since it had an all-male lyric. Loud thunder rolled while lightning flared and sizzled. Our fans fell back into an appreciative half circle while we let fly.

*Death and torture and murder and rape—*
*WE LIKE IT! WE LIKE IT!*
*Cutting and slashing and murder and looting,*
*Hacking and cracking and stabbing and shooting.*
*Blowing up slowing up showing up to kill*
*Arson and cursin' done with a will—*
*'Cause . . .*
*NOTHING'S TOO BAD FOR THE ENEMEEE . . .*
*Drinking and drinking and drinking and drinking*
*Shouting and cursing and lying and stinking*
*Chasing girls grabbing girls huggin' and kissin'*
*Showing girls all the things they been missin' . . .*

As can easily be imagined this delicate flower of a lyric really went down well with the troops. They were still cheering when there was a hissing rumble behind us and we turned to see that our transportation had arrived. Perhaps the locals were used to these things but it was really eye-bugging time for the tourists.

"Only for special occasions, special people," Ljotur said proudly.

We gaped in silence, lost for words. There were two of the vehicles, made of wood and decorated with gilt scrolls and strands of jewels. Each had a single wheel in front which was steered by a tiller. This was manned by the driver who rode high above. I looked at the closer one. A wide seat was in the middle and there were two wheels to the rear. All of which was pretty commonplace—not counting the pricey decoration —if you did not allow for the propulsion at the back. This was a shining metal tube, now crackling and emitting an occasional puff of smoke. I drew my attention away from it as the ornate door was thrown wide. I stepped in and seated myself on the soft cushions. Floyd and Steengo were ushered reverently into the other vehicle. Doors were slammed and Ljotur shouted a command to the drivers.

"You're off! Fuel on! *Frapu viajn startigilojn!* Drivers hit your starters!"

I saw now that there was a metal tank under my driver's seat. He reached down and opened a valve and I could hear the gurgle of liquid in the pipe. Then he stamped down on a pedal; the starter I guess.

No—it just started the starter. The pedal pulled on a cord that ran on pulleys to the rear of the chariot. This lifted and dropped a small hammer that banged the starter on the shoulder. This was an individual, dressed completely in black, who sat on a little platform slung behind the wheels. Not only dressed in black, but with blackened arms and face, his hair a burnt stubble. I soon found out why. Liquid was now dripping from the metal tube and the starter reached out and touched a match to it, jumped back as it ignited. A tongue of black smoke and flame leaped out to the rear, singeing the soldiers who weren't quick enough out of the way.

Now the starter was grinding away at a handle, presumably pumping air into the primitive jet. Within seconds the roar grew louder, the flame longer—and my Chariot of Fire shuddered and began to slowly roll forward. Very showy. Though it probably only got about a mile to a hundred gallons. I waved cheerfully to my fellow victims, who waved feebly and fearfully back. Relax Jim, sit back and enjoy the ride.

It was hard to do. I admit I did not see much of the passing scenery, being too involved with thoughts of survival. Nor did I relax until our little convoy had stopped and the blowtorch behind me was extinguished. The chariot's door swung open to the blast of discordant horns. I grabbed up my pack and stepped down onto a gray stepping block.

Which was resistant but soft. I turned and looked and saw that it was not a step at all but a man dressed in gray, kneeling on all fours. He rose and scurried off, along with another human footstep. Midgets, about as tall as my waist and almost as wide. My companions had reacted as I had, our eyes met but we said nothing.

"Greetings," a stentorian voice bellowed. "Welcome, welcome visitors to Paradise."

"Thanks much," I said to the tall and barrel-chested man who was draped in gold cloth. "Iron John, I presume?"

"Most flattering—but you presume wrongly. Musical guests, kindly follow me."

The trumpets blared again, then the trumpeters opened ranks. Three gray-clad men hurried up and took our packs. I started to resist, then made the reluctant decision that it would be all right. The reception we had received at the archway had been too spontaneous to be planned. Our gold-clad greeter bowed to us, then led the way. Towards the brick steps of a brick building.

If the Paradisians were short on building materials they certainly weren't bereft of architectural imagination. Tall pillars, capped with ornate capitals, rose up to support the archi-

trave of a complex entablature. Just like I had been taught in
Architecture 1. To either side tall windows opened onto wide
balconies. And all of this done in red brick.

"Looks great so far," Floyd said.

"Yes, great," I agreed. But I looked back to make sure the
porters with our packs were right behind us. And I still had
the concussion grenades in my pocket. No one ever got into
trouble by being prepared—as we used to say in the Boy
Sprouts.

Down a brick corridor over brick paving we went.
Through a brick doorway into a great and impressive room. It
was colorfully lit by the sunlight that streamed through the
ceiling-high, stained-glass windows. Colorful scenes were depicted there of armies marching, attacking, fighting, dying; the
usual thing. This motif was carried through to the walls which
were hung with tattered battle banners, shields and swords.
Robed men who stood about the room turned and nodded to
us as we entered. But our guide led us past them to the far wall
where there was an elevated throne, made of you-know-what,
on which was seated the tallest man I have ever seen.

Not only tall—but naked.

At least he would have been naked if he had not been
completely covered with rusty, reddish hair. His beard cas-
caded down his chest—which was covered as well with hair.
Arms and legs and, I couldn't help peeking when he stood,
hair all down his belly and crotch as well. This was all that was
visible since he was wearing a sort of jockstrap or sporran
woven out of, well possibly, his own hair. All of it the color of
rusty iron. I stepped forward and bowed a little bow.

"Iron John . . . ?"

"None other," he rumbled in a voice like distant thunder.
"Welcome Jim—and Floyd and Steengo. Welcome Stainless
Steel Rats. Your fame has gone before you."

Always good to meet a true fan. We all bowed now since

this was not the kind of reception you normally get. Bowed yet again as all in the room cheered lustily.

Iron John sat down again and crossed his legs. He either painted his toenails or they were naturally rusty. I let it pass since there were a lot more things I would like to know first.

"All here in Paradise were possessed of a great depression when you were arrested," he said. "Falsely of course?"

"Of course!"

"I thought so. But the galaxy's loss is our gain. We are pleased since we now have, you might say, a monopoly on your talents."

This had an ominous sound which I ignored for the moment, cocking an ear as he rumbled on.

"The galaxy is so filled with guilt, sorrow and wrong-headedness that we chose, out of disgust, not to watch most of what is disseminated by television. I am sure that it will cheer you to know that, since your arrest and incarceration, we have canceled normal programming and have been running recordings of your numbers, day and night. Now, soon, we will be happily blessed with the originals themselves!"

This was greeted by cries of enthusiasm and we replied with nods, grins and handshakes over our heads. When the shouts had died away old Rusty boomed out what they all wanted to hear.

"It is our hope that you will now—play for us!" More shouts. "What a pleasure to hear live our favorite favorite—'Nothing's Too Bad For the Enemy.' But while you are setting up we will broadcast a recording to warm up our nation-wide audience, to prepare them for your first live performance."

Which was not a bad idea since, although we could get going fast, their TV technicians were another thing altogether. Very much on the antique side. They dragged in arm-thick cables, antique-looking, homemade cameras and lights and other gear that belonged in a museum. While this was happening a screen dropped down from the ceiling and lit up with lively color when the back projector came on.

The recorded program did not have what might be called the galaxy's most inspiring opening. About a thousand sun-tanned bodybuilders drove heavy stakes into the ground with sledgehammers, backed by the thud of a beating drum. The drum died away but the hammers kept hammering silently as the voice-over spoke.

"Gentlemen of Paradise—we now bring you the special occasion that was announced a few minutes ago. I know that all of you, right across the land, are riveted to your sets. I think that we are going to get a hundred-percent rating on this one! So while The Stainless Steel Rats are warming up for their first-ever live performance here, we are privileged to play for you their special version of—'The Spaceship Way'!"

And it really was special. We watched ourselves attacking the song with our usual gusto, listened once again to those lovely lyrics . . .

> *Working on the engines, in the engine room,*
> *Wirin' and firin' an' waitin' for the boom.*
> *When the cannons blast like the sound of doom,*
> *You know you're a-sweatin' in the engine room.*
> *Captain on the bridge his fingers on the triggers*
> *All the guns loaded by the spaceship riggers.*
> *Swoopin' on the enemy, million miles an hour*
> *Callin' to the engine room for power, power, power.*
> *Power, Power, Power make the electrons whirl,*
> *Power, Power, Power—hear them protons swirl!*
> *Power, Power, Power will win the day—*
> *Power, Power, Power, that's the SPACESHIP WAY!*

We nodded and smiled with fixed grins. Good-quality picture, good sound as well. The audience was looking at the screen instead of at us for the moment. Floyd looked at me, then raised his extended index finger to the side of his head and rotated it in a quick little circle. The universal hand signal for insanity. I nodded glum agreement. I couldn't understand it either.

There we were on the screen playing on a familiar set, wearing our regular concert costumes. Only one thing was wrong.

Until this moment none of us had ever seen the tenor who was right there with us, singing the song.

Tenor?

It had always been sung in sensuous contralto by Madonette.

# CHAPTER 14

After the TV intro we played our number, pretty mechanically I must say. Not that our audience noticed, they were too carried away simply by being in the Presence. They swayed and waved their hands in the air and fought to keep silent. But when Iron John joined us in the "Power" chorus they cheered and howled and sang right along with him. When the last power had been overpowered they broke into lusty shouted applause that went on for a long, long time. Iron John smiled beneficently at this and finally stopped it with a raised russet finger. There was instant silence.

"I join you in your enthusiasm for our honored guests. But we must give them time to rest after their strenuous day. We will surely hear them sing for us again. You must remember they are with us now forever. It is their rare privilege to be admitted to Paradise as full citizens, to live until the end of time in our fair land."

More cries of masculine joy. We concealed our overwhelming pleasure at this life sentence and kept our silence as we packed up our instruments and handed them to the waiting servants. Our audience moved out, still throbbing slightly with musical passion.

"A moment please," Iron John said, waiting for the others to leave. When we were alone he touched a button at his side and the tall doors swung silently closed. "A fine song. We all enjoyed it."

"The Stainless Steel Rats aim only to please," I said.

"Wonderful." His smile vanished and he stared at us grimly. "There is one more thing you must do to please me. Your stay here will be a long one and we want you to be happy. You will make us all happy, yourselves included, if you show a certain selection in topics of conversation."

"What do you mean?" I asked—although I had a good notion of what he was leading up to.

"We are very satisfied here. Adjusted and secure. I do not wish to see that security threatened. You gentlemen come to our land from a very troubled outside world. The galaxy is at peace—or so you say. While ignoring the eternal war without end. The conflict of duality that we are free of here. You are the products of a society that is ego destroying instead of being ego building. You suffer from the negativity that blights lives, weakens cultures, sickens even the strongest. Do you know what I'm talking about?"

Neither Floyd nor Steengo answered so it was up to me. I nodded.

"We do. Although we might quibble with some of your conclusions the object of your attentions is quite clear. I can promise you that while we are enjoying your hospitality, neither I nor my associates will talk to anyone about the other sex. That is girls, women, females. It is a taboo topic. But, since you raised the issue I assume that you can discuss it . . ."

"No."

"Right, answer enough. We will therefore enjoy your hospitality and not spoil it."

"You are wise beyond your years, young Jim," he said, and a trace of a smile returned. "Now you must be tired. You will be shown to your quarters."

The doors opened, he turned away. End of interview. We strolled out as nonchalantly as we could. Old Goldy led us out as he had led us in, to some pretty luxurious, although still red brick, quarters. He turned on the TV, checked that the faucets worked in the bathroom, raised and lowered the curtains, then bowed himself out and closed the door. I touched my finger to my lips. Floyd and Steengo waited in twitching silence while I used the detector, borrowed from Tremearne, to sweep the room for bugs. After what we had seen on TV I had a great admiration for the electronics in this place.

"Nothing," I said.

"No women," Steengo said. "And we can't even talk about them."

"I can live with that for awhile," Floyd cut in. "But who was *that* singing our number?"

"That," I said, "was a very nifty example of some first-class electronic dubbing."

"But where did that joker come from?" Floyd said. "There I am playing right beside him—and I swear that I have never seen him before. Maybe we really did blow baksheesh and this whole planet is a drug-inspired nightmare!"

"Keep cool, keep calm. That guy was nothing but a bunch of electronic bytes and bits. Some really good techs digitalized that entire song, with all of us playing it. Then they animated a computer-generated male singer to follow all of Madonette's movements. Wrote her image out, wrote his in—then rerecorded the whole thing just as if it were going out live. Only with a him instead of a her."

"But why?" Steengo asked, dropping wearily into one of the deep lounges.

"Now you have asked the right question. And the answer is obvious. This side of Paradise is for men only. Not only haven't we seen any women here—but pretty obviously they have been edited out of TV and presumably everything else going. It's a real man's world. And don't say *why* again because I don't know. You saw how high that wall is when we were on our way here. And we know from views of the thing from space that the city is on *both* sides of the wall. So the women—if there are any women—might very well be on the other side."

No one said *why* again but that was the only thing on our minds. I stared at their worried faces and tried to think of something nice. I did. "Madonette," I said.

"What about her?" Steengo asked.

"We've got to tell her what has happened." I stuck my thumb in my ear and addressed my pinkie. "Jim calling Madonette. Are you on-line?"

*"Very much so."*

*"I read you as well,"* Tremearne said tinnily from my thumbnail.

I outlined the events of the day. Said *over* and awaited any reaction. Madonette gasped, nor could I blame her, but Tremearne was all business as usual.

*"You are doing well on your side of the wall. Is it time for Madonette to check out her side?"*

"Not yet, not until we have a few answers to an awful lot of questions."

*"Agreed—but only for now. What have you discovered about the artifact?"*

"Negative so far. Give us a break, Captain. Don't you think that getting in here, pressing the flesh and doing a gig is enough for one day?" The silence lengthened. "Yes, sir, right you are—it's not enough. One alien artifact coming up. Over and out."

I pulled my finger out of my ear, wiped the earwax off of it, stared gloomily into space.

"How do we find it?" Floyd asked.

"I haven't the slightest idea. I just said that to get Tremearne off my neck."

"I know how we start," Steengo said. I launched a quizzical look in his direction.

"First the MIPSC and now this. Our humble harp player reveals hidden depths." He nodded and smiled.

"All those years laboring for the League perhaps. Didn't the ancient gladhander at the gate tell us that there would be a market at dawn tomorrow?"

"His very words," Floyd said. "But so what? The artifact is long gone from the market."

"Of course. But the merchants aren't. There is a good chance that whoever bought the thing might still be there."

"A genius!" I applauded. "Behind those gray hairs lies even grayer gray matter that knows how to think!"

He nodded acceptance. "I never did enjoy retirement. What's next, boss Jim?"

"Grab Goldy. Show strong interest in the market. Have him lay on a guide to take us there when it opens in the morning . . ."

As though speaking his name had been a summons; bugles sounded, the door opened, our gilt-garbed guardian came in.

"A summons for you, oh lucky ones. Iron John will see you in the Veritorium. Come!"

We went—since we had little choice. For a change Goldy was not in a chatty mood; waving off our queries with a flick of his hand. More corridors, more bricks—and another door. It opened into misty darkness. Stumbling and barking our ankles we made our way to a row of waiting chairs, sat down as instructed. It was even darker when Goldy closed the door behind him as he left.

"I don't like this," Floyd muttered, muttering for all of us.

"Patience," I said for lack of any more intelligent answer, then nervously squeezed my knuckles until they cracked. There was a movement of air in the darkness and a growing glow. Iron John swam into view, a blown-up image really. He pointed at us.

"The experience that you are about to have is vital to your

existence. Its memory will sustain you and uplift you and will never be forgotten. I know that you will be ever grateful and I accept your tearful thanks in advance. This is the experience that will change you, develop you, enrich you. Welcome, welcome, to the first day of the rest of your new and fulfilling lives."

As his image faded I coughed to cover the grunt of suspicion that this old bushwah evoked. Never try to con a conman. I settled my rump more comfortably in the chair and prepared to be entertained.

As soon as it started I could see that the holofilm was very professionally made. I appreciated that the young, the gullible —or the just plain stupid—would be very impressed by it. The mist churned, the russet light grew brighter and I was suddenly in the midst of the scene.

*The king watched in silence as the group of armed men walked warily into the forest and disappeared from sight among the trees. Outwardly he was patient as he waited, although he reached up and touched his crown from time to time as though reassuring himself that it was still there, that he was still king. A very long time later he stiffened, turned his head and listened as slow footsteps shuffled through the thick leaves below the trees. But no warrior appeared, just the thick and twisted figure of his jester, headdress bobbling, lips moist with flecked saliva.*

*"What did you see?" the king asked at last.*

*"Gone, Majesty. All gone. Just like all of those who have gone before. Vanished among the trees around the lake. None returned."*

*"None ever return," the king said, sorrow and defeat dragging him down. He stood that way, unknowing, unseeing as a young man appeared and strode towards him; a silent gray dog walked at his side. The jester, jaw agape, spittle pendulous, backed away as the stranger approached.*

*"Why do you grieve, oh king?" he asked in a light and clear voice.*

*"I grieve for there is part of the forest in my kingdom where men do go—but none return. They go in tens and twenties—but none is ever seen again."*

*"I will go," the young man said, "but I will go alone."*

*He snapped his fingers and, without another word being spoken, man and dog walked off into the forest. Beneath the trees and pendant mosses, around the hedges and nodding cattails to the edge of a dark pond. The young man stopped to look at it—and a hand, sudden and dripping, rose from the water and seized the dog. Pulled it beneath the surface. The ripples died away and the surface was still.*

*The young man did not cry or flee, just nodded.*

*"This must be the place," he said.*

The darkness faded and light returned. Iron John was gone, the chamber was empty. I looked at Floyd who seemed just as bewildered as I was.

"Did I miss the point somehow?" I asked.

"I feel sorry for the dog," Floyd said. We both looked at Steengo who was nodding thoughtfully.

"That's only the beginning," he said. "You'll understand what is happening when you see the rest."

"You wouldn't like to, maybe, explain just what you are talking about?"

Steengo shook his head in a solemn no. "Later, perhaps. But I don't think I will have to. You will see for yourselves."

"You've seen this holoflick before?" Floyd asked.

"No. But I have read my mythology. It's better that you see the rest before we talk about it."

I started to protest, shut my mouth. Realized that there was no point in probing further. The door opened and our guide reappeared.

"Just the man we are looking for," I said, remembering our earlier decision. "We have heard, from reliable sources, that there is to be an outdoor market at dawn tomorrow."

"Your sources are correct. Tomorrow is the tenth day and that is market day. Always on the tenth day because the nomads remember by marking a finger each day with soot until all fingers are . . ."

"Right, thanks. I can count to ten without dirty fingers. My fellow musicians and I would like to visit this market—is this possible?"

"You have but to ask, great Jim of The Stainless Steel Rats."

"I've asked. Can someone show us the way in the morning?"

"'Tis more fit that you use the Chariots of Fire . . ."

"I agree, more fit. But more fit that we be fit. Walking is a wonderful exercise."

"Then walk you shall, if that is your desire. An escort will be provided. It is now the hour of dining and a banquet has been prepared in your honor. Will you be so kind as to follow me?"

"Lead on, my friend. As long as it is not polpettone again we are your avid customers."

As we followed him out I discovered that my fingers had a life of their own. Or, more probably, were being twitched into activity by my worried subconscious. They flicked over the computer controls and the glowing numbers appeared before me.

Nineteen and a pulsing red eleven.

Eleven days to go. The morning market had better produce something.

# CHAPTER 15

"It is going to be such a lovely day," the voice said.

Each word shot through my head like a rusty arrow, grating and scraping against the growing headache that was throbbing there. I opened one eye blurrily and bright light added to the pain. I had only enough energy to twist my lips into a surly snarl as our gold-clad host flitted about our quarters. Opening curtains, picking up discarded clothing, generally being as obnoxious as possible at this predawn hour. Only when I heard the outer door slam did I crawl from the bed, turn off the searing lights, stumble on all fours to my pack where it rested against the wall. On the third fumbling attempt I managed to open it and click out a Sobering Effect pill. I swallowed it dry and sat motionlessly while I waited for its beneficent chemicals to seep through my fractured body.

"What was in that green beer?" Floyd said hoarsely, then began to cough. Moaning in agony between coughs as his aching head was kicked about. My headache was seeping away so I clicked out a pill for him and walked unsteadily across to his bed of pain.

"Swallow. This. Will. Help."

"Quite a party last night," Steengo said benevolently, joined fingers resting comfortably on the ample bulge of his stomach.

"Die," Floyd gasped, unsteady fingers groping for the pill. "And burn painfully in hell forever. Plus one day."

"A bit hungover are we?" Steengo asked cheerfully. "I

suppose there is good reason, considering the length of the nights here. Their parties must go on forever. Or maybe it just seems that way. Eat a bit, sleep a bit. Eat a bit, drink a bit. Or maybe more than a bit. I thought that the beer tasted a little on the nasty side. So I only had one. But the meat courses! Tremendous, vegetables, good gravy, liked the bread and red sauce, plus . . ."

His voice died away as Floyd crawled out of bed and staggered, groaning, from the room.

"You are cruel," I said, smacking my dry lips together and feeling a little better.

"Not cruel. Just pointing out a few truths. This mission first. Overdrinking, hangovers and Technicolor yawns saved for our victory celebration."

There was nothing I could say. He was right.

"Message received," I said, reaching for my clothes. "The quiet life and plenty of rest and raw vegetables. Think positive."

Dawn brightened the window. A new day. Ten days to deadline. I was thinking negative and I shook myself like a wet dog and tried to shrug off the mood. "Let's go to the fair."

When we emerged from the BOQ, Sergeant Ljotur was waiting for us. He snapped to attention and gave a mighty salute—as did the squad of soldiers from the gate guard that he had brought with him.

"We take you to the market!" he called out. "These men are all volunteers, eagerly happy to carry any purchases finest musicians in galaxy may make."

"Greatly appreciated. Lead on," I said as we stepped out briskly on the red brick road.

The sun was a glowing crimson disk on the horizon when we reached the market. The Fundamentaloid nomads must have been early risers because everything was in great swing already. And gory too; I thought I heard a low moan from

Floyd, but the baaing and farting of the sheots tended to drown out most other sounds. Complain they might as the butchered carcasses of their late companions were unloaded from their backs. But there had to be more than a meat market here; eyes averted we hurried past the sanguineous display.

Now bearded nomads solicited our attention in pleading voices, pointing out the attractions of their wares. Which weren't that attractive. Tired-looking vegetables, crude clay pots, piles of dried sheot chips for the barbecue.

"Pretty grim," Floyd said.

"Not important," I told him, jerking my thumb towards the strolling customers. "They are the ones that we are interested in." I took out the photographs of the artifact that we were looking for and passed one to each of my companions. "Find out if any of the Paradisians have seen this."

"We don't just spring it on them?" Steengo said doubtfully.

"You're right. We don't. During the sleepless hours of the night I worked up a cover story. It goes this way, something close to the truth. The nomads found this thing in a streambed after a flash flood. Tried to trade it to the keepers of the Pentagon who have a strict policy of noncommunication. However it was photographed when presented and only later was it recognized as an archeological artifact of possible interest."

"Reasonable," Steengo said doubtfully. "But what are we doing with the photos?"

"Given to us when we were booted out of the place. Hints made of rewards, possible remission of sentence, lots of fedha. With great reluctance we agreed to look for the thing since, simply, what have we got to lose?"

"Thin but plausible," Floyd said. "Let's give it a try."

There was no difficulty talking to the Paradisians; if anything it was hard to get rid of them once approached. How they loved The Stainless Steel Rats! Soon I had a string of adoring fans trailing behind me—along with most of the squad of guards. Everyone wanted to help: none of them knew a thing. But—one name kept cropping up during the questioning. Sjonvarp.

Steengo pushed through the crowd and held up the now dog-eared photograph. "Still nothing. But a couple of them said to ask Sjonvarp. Who seems to be the top trader around here."

"I heard the same thing. Grab Floyd. He must be recovering because I saw him looking at the fermented sheot-milk stand. Bring him here before he makes a mistake that he will long remember."

Sjonvarp was easy enough to find, with countless fingers pointing us the way. He was a tall and solidly-built man with iron-gray hair. His stern face broke into a smile when he turned to see who had called out his name.

"The Stainless Steel Rats in the flesh! I am trebly blessed!"

We hummed two bars of "All Alone" followed by a brisk buck and wing. Which elicited a round of applause from the spectators and a broader smile from Sjonvarp.

"Such rhythm and beauty!" he said.

"We sing 'em the way you like it," I said. "It is told in the market that you are the master-trader in these parts."

"I am. Pleased to make your acquaintances, Jim, Floyd and Steengo."

"Likewise. If you have a moment I have a picture here I would like you to look at." I hit the high points of our spiel as I passed the pic over. He only half listened, but did put all of his attention on the photo. Turning it around at arm's length, squinting farsightedly to make it out.

"Of course! I thought so." He handed it back to me. "Some markets ago, I forget exactly how many, one of these odorous simpletons traded it to one of my assistants. We buy anything that might be of scientific interest for the specialists to examine. It didn't look like much. But I gave it to old Heimskur anyway."

"Well that takes care of that then," I said, tearing the photo up and dropping the pieces. "We're doing our concert tonight—I can get you a ticket if you want one."

The artifact was instantly forgotten—as I hoped, although it took some time for us to extract ourselves from the attentive embrace of our fans. Only by saying that it was rehearsal time did we manage to break away.

"Don't we look for the thing any more?" Floyd asked worriedly. A good musician, but I think drink was eroding his brain cells.

"We have the man's name," Steengo said. "That's what we look into next."

"How?" Floyd asked, still suffering from semi-paralysis of the neural network.

"Any way we can," I told him. "Make friends. Drop names. Drop Heimskur's name among the others. We find out who he is and what he does. Now, as we stroll, I'll report in."

Tremearne and Madonette listened carefully to my report. He overed and outed but she stayed to chat.

*"Jim, it's time I left my hole in the wall and visited the other half of the city. It must be safe . . ."*

"We hope that—but we don't know that. And there is no point in your taking any chances as long as the thing we are looking for is here. Enjoy the break. And don't do a thing until we find out more here."

We found lunch waiting in our quarters. Fruit and slices of cold meatloaf on silver plates, covered with crystal domes.

"Great!" Floyd said, chomping down a slice.

"Probably minced sheot shank," Steengo said, suddenly gloomy.

"Food's food and I never consider the source." Floyd reached for another slice just as our golden greeter appeared.

"A pleasure to see you musical Rats enjoying yourself. When you have eaten your fill I have a request for the presence of Rat Jim."

"Who wants me?" I asked suspiciously through a mouthful of sweet pulp.

"All will be revealed." He put his index finger along his nose, winked and rolled his eyes. Which silent communication I assumed meant something like you'll find out soon enough. I had no choice. And I had lost my appetite. I wiped my fingers on a damp cloth and followed him yet another time.

Iron John was waiting for me at the door of the Veritorium where we had all seen the puzzling holoflic.

"Come with me, Jim," he said with a deep voice like distant thunder. "Today you will see and understand all of the revelation."

"I'll get the others . . ."

"Not this time, Jim." His hand closed gently but firmly onto my shoulder and I had little choice but to go along with him. "You are wise beyond your years. An old head on a young body. Therefore you are the one who will be helped the most by your understanding of this mystery that is no mystery. Come."

He sat me down but did not join me; yet I was aware of his presence close by me in the darkness. The mist roiled and cleared and I was once again by the lake.

*There was only silence in the forest around the dark pond. As the last ripple died away the young man turned and left without looking back. Trod the dead leaves beneath the trees until he emerged and saw the king before him.*

*"There is something I must do," he told the king, nor would he say any more. The king saw that the man's dog was gone— but the man himself was unharmed. He had many questions but did not know how to speak them. Instead he followed the young*

*man back to the castle. In the courtyard the young man looked
around, then spotted a large leathern bucket.*

*"I need that," he said.*

*"Take it." The king dismissed him with a wave of his hand.
"Remember I have helped you. One day you must tell me what
you found in the woods."*

*The young man turned in silence and made his way, alone,
back to the dark pond. There he dipped the bucket into the
water and hurled its contents into the ditch nearby. Another and
another. He did not stop but worked steadily at bailing out the
pond. It was hard, slow work. Yet the sun never set, the light
never changed, the young man never stopped.*

*After a great period of time the water was almost gone and
something large was revealed lying in the mud on the bottom of
the pond. The young man kept emptying the water until he
revealed a tall man who was covered with reddish hair, like
rusty iron, from head to foot. The large man's eyes opened and
he looked at the young man. Who beckoned to him. With a
heaving shake the rusty man rose from the pond's bottom and
followed the young man away from the pond and through the
woods.*

*To the castle of the king. All of the soldiers and retainers fled
when they appeared and the king alone stood before them.*

*"This is Iron John," the young man said. "You must im-
prison him in an iron cage here in the courtyard. If you lock the
cage and give the key to your queen the forest will be safe again
for those who walk through it."*

*Mist rose and darkened the scene. It was the end.*

The red-furred hand was heavy on Jim's shoulder—but it
did not bother him.

"Now you understand," Iron John said, newfound warmth
in his voice. "Now you can release Iron John. Welcome, Jim,
welcome."

I wanted to say that I felt more confusion than comprehension. That I was experiencing something, yet not understanding it. Instead of speaking my feelings aloud I suddenly found that my eyes were brimming with tears. I did not know why—although I knew that they were nothing to be ashamed of.

Iron John smiled at me and, with a great finger, wiped the tears from my damp cheeks.

# CHAPTER 16

"What was all that about?" Floyd asked when I returned to our quarters. He was jazzing with his trombonio, a complex and gleaming collection of golden tubes and slides, which made some very interesting sounds indeed. Most of them, regrettably, of an ear-destroying nature.

"More training film," I said, as nonchalantly as I could. I was surprised to hear a certain quaver in my voice as I spoke. Floyd tootled on, unaware of it, but Steengo who appeared to be asleep on the couch opened one eye.

"Training film? You mean more about the pool in the forest?"

"You got it in one."

"Did you find out what was in the pool? The thing that dragged the dog down?"

"A stupid story," Floyd said, and tootled a little fast riff. "Although I do feel sorry for the dog."

"It wasn't a real dog," Steengo said. He looked at me, seemed to be waiting for me to speak, but I clamped my jaw shut and turned away. "Nor was it a real pool."

"What do you mean?" I asked, looking at him.

"Mythology, my dear Jim. And rites of passage. It was Iron John at the bottom of the pool, wasn't it?"

I jumped as though I had been zapped with an electric shock. "It was! But—how did you know that?"

"I told you I read my mythology. But the thing that really

disturbs me—not this training film as you call it—is the fact that Iron John is here in the flesh, solid and hairy."

"You've lost me," Floyd said, looking from one to the other of us. "A little explanation is very much in order."

"It is," Steengo said, swinging his feet around so he sat up straight on the couch. "Mankind invents cultures—and cultures invent myths to justify and explain their existence. Prominent among these are the myths and ceremonies of the rites of passage for boys. The passage from boyhood to manhood. This is the time when the boy is separated from his mother and the other women. In some primitive cultures the boys go and live with the men—and never see their mothers again."

"No big loss," Floyd muttered. Steengo nodded.

"You heard that, Jim. In all cultures mothers try to shape sons in their female image. For their own good. The boys resist —and the rite of passage helps this resistance. There is always symbolism involved, because symbols are a way to represent the myths that underlie every culture."

I thought about this; my head hurt. "Sorry, Steengo, but you left me behind completely with that one. Explanation?"

"Of course. Let's stay with Iron John. You have just said that you didn't understand it—yet I think that it affected you emotionally."

I started to protest, to lie—then stopped. Why lie? I tried not to lie to myself, ever. This was a good moment to apply that rule.

"You're right. It got to me—and I don't know why . . ."

"Myths deal with emotions, not facts. Let's look at the symbols. Did the young man bail out the pool and find Iron Hans, or Iron John at the bottom?"

"That's exactly what happened."

"Who do you think Iron John is? In the story I mean, not the one walking around here. But before you answer that— who do you think the young man in the story was?"

"That's not too hard to figure out. Whoever the story was aimed at, whoever was watching it. In this case, since I was there alone, I guess it must have been me."

"You are correct. So in the myth you, and every other young man, are looking for something in the pool, and have to work very very hard with the bucket to find it. Now we come to Iron John, the hairy man at the bottom of the pool. Is it a real man?"

"No, of course it couldn't be. The man at the bottom of the pool has to be a symbol. Part of a myth. A symbol of manhood, maleness. The primitive male that lies beneath the surface in all of us."

"Bang-on, Jim," he said in a low voice. "The story is trying to tell you that when a man, not a boy, looks deep inside himself, if he looks far down and for long enough, works hard enough, he will find the ancient hairy man within himself."

Floyd stopped playing and his jaw gaped. "You guys been smoking something I don't know about."

"Not smoking," Steengo said. "Sipping at the font of ancient wisdom."

"Do you believe this myth?" I asked Steengo. He shrugged.

"Yes and no. Yes, the process of growing up is a difficult one and anything that helps the process is a good thing. Yes, myths and coming-of-age ceremonies help prepare boys, giving them the assurances they need in the transition from boy to man. But that is as far as I will go. I say *no* resoundingly to a myth manifest as reality. Iron John alive and well and leading the pack. This is a fractured society here, without women and without even the knowledge of women. Not good. Quite sick."

I was uneasy at this. "I don't agree all the way. I was affected very strongly by watching that story. And I am a very hard guy to con. This got to me."

"It should have—because it was dealing with the very stuff of personality and self. I have a feeling, Jim, that yours was not the happiest of childhoods . . ."

"Happy!" I laughed at the thought. "You try growing up on a porcuswine farm surrounded by bucolic peasants who are not much brighter than their herds."

"And that includes your father and mother?"

I started to answer warmly, saw what he was doing and where this was going. I shut up. Floyd shook the spittle from his so-called musical instrument and broke the silence.

"I still feel sorry for the dog," he said.

"Not a real dog," Steengo said, turning away from me. "A symbolic dog like everything else you saw. The dog is your body, the thing you order around, *sit up, beg.*"

Floyd shook his head in amazement. "Too deep for me. Like that pool. If I could change the subject from theory to fact for just a moment—what's next on the agenda?"

"Finding Heimskur, of course, so we can find out if he still has the artifact," I said, happily putting this other matter aside. "Any suggestions?"

"Brain empty," Floyd said. "Sorry. That hangover never really went away."

"I'm glad some of us didn't drink," Steengo said, a sudden edge of irritation to his voice.

For personal reasons I was happy to hear it, glad that he was still human; he came on pretty strong with the myth stuff. Forget this for awhile. I ticked off on my fingers. "We have only two choices. Hint around about him and gather what information we can. Or blurt right out that we want to see him. Personally, I'm all for the blurting since there is a kind of time limit on this investigation." Like ten days to the grim reaper. "Let's ask Goldy, our majordomo. He seems to know everything else."

"Let me do it," Steengo said, standing and stretching. "I'll talk to him like an old buddy and work the conversation around to science and scientists. And Heimskur. Be right back."

Floyd watched him go, tooting a little march in time with his footsteps. "This Iron John stuff sort of gets to you," he said after the door had closed.

"Yes—and that's the worst part. I don't know why I'm bothered."

"Women. I had six sisters and there were two aunts who lived with us. I had no brothers. I never think about women except one at a time in the right situation."

Before I had to listen to one more boring macho tale about the right situation I excused myself and went for a jog. Returned sweating nicely, did some pushups and situps, then went for a wash. Steengo was there when I came out. Shaking his joined hands over his head when I lifted a quizzical eyebrow.

"Success. Heimskur is head of the bunch who Labor in the Cause of Science, or so Veldi says."

"Veldi . . . ?"

"The doorman here. He does have a name after all. From what he says I get the feeling that this is a pretty stratified society with everyone in their correct place. Great respect is given to the scientist. Veldi was more than respectful when he talked about them because they appear to be the ones pretty much in charge."

"Great. How do we get to meet Heimskur?"

"We wait patiently," Steengo said and looked at his watch. "Because any moment our transportation will be here to take us to his august presence."

"Not the Chariots of Fire again!" Floyd groaned.

"No. But something that sounds just as ominous. A Transport of Delight . . ."

Before we had time to dwell too long on that thought there was a brisk knocking and gold-clad Veldi threw the door open.

"Gentlemen—this way if you please."

We walked heads high and strong. Hiding any qualms we might have had. Though we shuddered to a halt when we saw what was awaiting us.

"Your Transport of Delight," Veldi said proudly, waving magnanimously in the direction of what could only be a land-locked lifeboat.

It was snow-white, clinker-built, with a stub mast festooned with flags, white wheels just visible tucked under the keel below. A uniformed officer looked down from the rail above, saluted, gave a signal—and the rope ladder clattered down to our feet.

"All aboard," I said as I led the way.

Cushioned divans awaited us while attendants beckoned and held out jars of cool drink. As soon as we were seated the officer signaled again and the drummer in the bow whirred his sticks in a rapid drumroll—then shifted to his bass drum. As the first, methodical boom boomed out the Transport of Delight shuddered. Then began to roll slowly forward.

"A galley—without slaves or oars," Floyd said.

"Plenty of slaves," I said as a wave of masculine perspiration wafted up from the funnel-shaped vent beside me. "But instead of oars they are grinding away at gears or some such, to turn the wheels."

"No complaints," Steengo said, sipping at his wine. "Not after the Chariots of Fire."

We rolled ponderously between the buildings, nodding at the bystanders and occasionally giving a royal flick of the hand at some of our cheering fans. We moved on through what appeared to be a residential quarter and beyond it into a park-like countryside. Our road wove between the trees, past a row of ornamental fountains to ponderously stop before an immense glass-walled building. A party of elegantly dressed ancients awaited us. Led by the most ancient of them all,

white-clad and standing firmly erect. But his face was wrinkled
beyond belief. I clambered down the ladder and dropped before him.

"Do I address the noble Heimskur?"

"You do. And of course you are Jim of the Rats. Welcome,
welcome all."

There was plenty of handshaking and glad cries of joy before Heimskur broke off the reception and led me into the
glass building.

"Welcome," he said, "doubly welcome. To the College of
Knowledge from whence all good things flow. If you will follow me I will explain our labors to you. Since you gentlemen
come from the surging, mongrel worlds outside our peaceful
boundaries you will surely appreciate how the application of
intelligence makes our society such a happy and peaceful
world. No strife, no differences, a place for everyone and everyone in their place. Down this way are the Phases of Physics,
the Caverns of Chemistry. There the Avenues of Agriculture,
next to them the Meadows of Medicine, while just beyond is
the Museum of Mankind."

"Museum?" I inquired offhandedly. "I simply love muse-
ums."

"Then you must see ours. It charts the difficulties through
which we passed before coming here, a rite of passage and of
cleansing, before we found safe haven on this world. Here we
grew and prospered and the record is clear for all to see."

And pretty boring if not just downright preposterous.
Cleaner than clean, whiter than white. The only thing missing
were the halos on the saints who had accomplished so much
good.

"Inspirational," I said when we finally reached the end of
the exhibition.

"It is indeed."

"And down this way?"

"The museum for students. Biologists can examine the plant life of our planet, geologists the strata and the schist."

"Archeologists?"

"Alas, very little. The crudest of artifacts left by the long-dead indigenes who first settled here."

"May we?"

"By all means. You see—fire sticks and crude pottery. A hand ax, a few arrow points. Scarcely worth preserving were we not so faithful to our role as recorders and archivists."

"Nothing more?"

"Nothing."

I dug the photograph from an inside pocket, took a deep breath—and passed it over.

"You may have heard that the warders in the Pentagon promised us favors if we helped them find this?"

"Did they indeed? I would believe nothing they said."

He took the photograph and blinked at it, handed it back. "Just like them to lie and cause trouble for no reason."

"Lie?"

"About this. It was brought here. I examined it myself. Not indigenous at all, couldn't possibly be. Probably something broken off an old spaceship. Meaningless and worthless. Gone now."

"Gone?" I fought to keep the despair from my voice.

"Discarded. Gone from Paradise. Non-existent. Men have no need of such rubbish therefore it is gone forever. Forget the worthless item Jim and we shall talk of far more interesting things. Music. You must tell me—do you write your own lyrics . . . ?"

# CHAPTER 17

We were very silent on our return trip, scarcely aware of the manifold pleasures that rode with us in our Transport of Delight. Only behind the closed doors of our quarters did we let go. I nodded appreciatively as I listened while Floyd swore blasphemously and scatologically; he had a fine turn of phrase and went on for a long time without repeating himself.

"And I double that," I said when lack of breath forced him to subside. "We have indeed been hard done by."

"We have," Steengo agreed. "But we have also been lied to."

"What do you mean?"

"I mean that Heimskur was selling us a line of old camel cagal. More than half of his so-called history of science and nature was pure propaganda for the troops. If we can't believe him about that—how can we believe him when he shovels a lot of bushwah about the artifact? Do you remember his last words?"

"No."

"Neither do I. But I hope someone does. I imagine that you didn't notice it—but I was doing a lot of head-scratching and nose-picking while we were doing that tour."

Floyd wasn't being bright today and gaped at the news. I smiled and put my index finger into my ear. "Come in ear in the sky. Do you read me?"

*"No but I hear you,"* Captain Tremearne said through my fingernail.

"Good. But more important—did you listen in to our guided tour?"

*"All of it. Very boring. But I recorded it anyway, the way you asked."*

"The way Steengo asked—credit where credit is due. Would you be so kind as to play back the last speech about the artifact."

*"Coming up."* After some clattering and high-pitched voices whizzing by our aged guide sounded forth.

*"Discarded. Gone from Paradise. Non-existent. Men have no need of such rubbish therefore it is gone forever."*

I copied it down and got it right after a couple of repeats. "That's it. Thanks."

"There," Steengo said, tapping the paper. "Weasel wording. That tricky old devil was playing with us, knowing that we had some reason to be interested in the thing. He never said destroyed, not once. Discarded? That means it might be still around someplace. Gone from Paradise—could be anywhere else on this planet. But I particularly like the bit about men having no need for the thing." He smiled a smile like a poker player laying down five Aces.

"If *men* have no need for it—what about women?"

"Women?" I felt my jaw hanging open and closed it with a clack. "What about them? There are only men here?"

"How right you are. And right on the other side of the town wall is—what? I'm betting on women. Either that or an awful lot of cloning is going on in this place. I'll bet on nature and some kind of connection through the wall."

My jawphone buzzed and Tremearne's voice echoed inside my sinuses. *"I agree with Steengo. And so does Madonette. She's already on her way along the wall to the city and will report as soon as she finds out anything."*

I started to protest, realized the futility, kept my mouth shut. "It figures," I said. "The gang in charge here lie about everything else—so lying about the artifact just comes naturally. We'll have to wait . . ."

I shut up as Veldi knocked quietly, then opened the door. "Good news!" he announced, eyes glowing with passion. "Iron John has chosen to speak to The Stainless Steel Rats—in the Veritorium itself. An honor above all other honors. Hurry, gentlemen. But first brush your clothing and, with the exception of heroically-bearded Floyd, diple the five o'clock shadow now gracing your musical jaws. What pleasures do await you!"

Pleasures better lived without. But this was a royal command and no way to get around it. I took a bit of diple-fast and rubbed my jaw smooth, combed my hair and tried not to scowl at myself in the mirror. I was the last to emerge and we boarded the Transport of Delight in silence, rolled ponderously to our destiny.

"I wonder why all three of us?" Steengo said, sipping his glass of chilled wine. "Last time it was you alone at the training-film session, wasn't it, Jim?"

"I have no idea," I said, wanting to change the subject. Nor was I too pleased with his light-hearted attitude. I tried to think about Madonette going in alone to the other city, but my thoughts kept trundling back to Iron John. What was going to happen now?

When we entered the Veritorium I was surprised at how big it really was. It was better lit now and I saw that rows of seats reached up in a semicircle. They were all filled now— with the oldest collection of Paradisians I had seen so far. Bald heads and gray hair, wrinkles and toothless jaws.

Iron John himself stepped forward to greet us. "You are all truly welcome here—and these seats are for you." They were three of the best in the front row—separated from the others. "You are our honored guests, musical Stainless Steel Rats. This occasion is a special one—specially so for young James diGriz. You are the youngest man here, Jim, and very soon you will find out why. Your companions will, I am sure, watch with pleasure. Not only pleasure but I sincerely hope that they will learn by observation. Now we begin . . ."

Cued by his words the lights died and darkness filled the Veritorium. Footsteps sounded in the darkness, and there was a small laugh. Light appeared and I saw the small boy hurry forward, stumbling a bit under the weight of the box he was carrying. He put it down and opened the lid, took out a top that started spinning when he touched its switch. Then he took out a tray of blocks, started to build a tower with them. When it was high enough he turned to take another toy out of the box. He was a very concentrated, very intense young boy, about eight years old. He rummaged deeper in the box, then looked around with a childish frown.

"Don't hide, teddy," he said. Looked behind the toy box, then into it again and then—with sudden determination—turned and hurried off. He vanished from sight but I could hear his footsteps going away, stopping. Then coming back. Carrying a teddy bear. A commonplace, slightly worn, very ordinary teddy bear. He propped it against the toy box and started building a second tower from the blocks.

The scene grew lighter and I realized we were back in the castle courtyard. The boy was alone—or was he? Something was there in the darkness, a shape that grew clearer.

It was an iron cage and, sitting silently, inside it was Iron John. The boy shouted and knocked over the block towers, ran to pick up the strewn blocks. Looked at Iron John, then away. The cage and its occupant must be a familiar sight to him.

Nothing else happened. The boy played, Iron John watched him in silence. Yet there was an electric tension in the air that made it hard to breathe. I knew that something vitally important was about to happen, and when the boy reached again into the toy box I found myself leaning forward.

When he took the small golden ball from the box I realized that I had been holding my breath; I let it out with a gasp. Nor was I the only one for around me in the darkness there were echoes of my gasp.

The ball bounced and rolled and the boy laughed with pleasure.

Then he threw it once, harder than intended, and it rolled and rolled. Through the bars of the iron cage to stop at Iron John's feet.

"My ball," the boy said. "Give it back."

"No," Iron John said. "You must unlock this cage and let me out. Then you will have your golden ball back."

"Locked," the boy said.

Iron John nodded. "Of course. But you know how to find the key."

The boy was shaking his head *no* as he backed away.

"Where is the key?" the man in the cage asked, but the boy was gone. "Where is the key? But you are only a boy. Perhaps you are too young to know where the key is. You must be older to find the key."

There were murmurs of agreement from the invisible audience. It was very important to find the key, I knew that. The key . . .

It was then that I became aware that Iron John was looking at me. He was there in the cage; it wasn't a holoflic. He looked at me and nodded.

"Jim, I'll bet you know where the key is. You are no longer a boy. You can find it—*now*."

His voice was a goad. I was on my feet, walking forward to the box of toys. My foot touched a block and it rattled aside.

"The key is in the toy box," I said, but I didn't believe the words even as I spoke them. I looked at Iron John who shook his head *no.*

"Not in the box."

I looked down again and realized that I did know where the key was. I raised my eyes to Iron John and he nodded solemnly. "See you *do* know where the key to the cage is. You can let me out now, Jim. Because you know the key is there. Inside . . ."

"Teddy," I said.

"Teddy. Not a real bear. Teddies are for children and you are no longer a child. Inside teddy."

I reached out, blinked away the tears that were blurring my vision, seized up the toy, felt the soft fabric between my fingers. Heard a loud voice that slashed the silence.

"Not quite right, Jim, not right. The key is not there—it has to be *under your mother's pillow!*"

Steengo had come forward to join me, had to shout the last words to be heard over the roar of voices.

"Mother doesn't want her son to leave her. She hides the key to the Iron man's cage under her pillow. The son must steal the key . . ."

The shouting voices drowned him out. Then it went dark in an instant and someone ran into me knocking me down. I tried to stand, to call out, but a hard foot walked on my hand. I shouted aloud at the sudden pain but my voice went unheard in the clamor. Someone else jarred into me and the darkness became even more intense.

"Jim—are you all right? Can you hear me?"

Floyd's face was just above mine, looking worried. Was I all right? I didn't know. I was in bed, must have been asleep. Why was he waking me?

Then I remembered and sat upright, grabbed his arms.

"The Veritorium! It got dark, something happened. I can't remember—"

"I'm not much help because I can't either. It seemed like a good show. Hard to follow the plot but you were in it, do you remember that?" I nodded. "Seemed to be enjoying yourself, although you didn't look happy about tearing the stuffing out of the teddy bear. That's when Steengo joined you onstage and all the fun started. Or stopped. It all gets vague about that time."

"Where's Steengo?"

"You tell me. I saw him last on the stage. I was sleeping myself, just woke up. Looked around, no Steengo. Found you here snoring away and I gave you a shake."

"If he's not here . . ."

A muted knock sounded at the door, and a moment later it opened and Veldi looked in.

"Gentlemen, a happy good morning to you both. I thought I heard your voices and hoped you would be awake. I bring you a message from your friend . . ."

"Steengo—you've seen him?"

"Indeed I did. We had a friendly chat before you awoke. Then, before he left, he made this recording. Told me to give it to you. Told me you would understand."

He placed a small recorder on the table, stepped back. "The green button is to play, red to stop." Then he was gone.

"A message?" Floyd asked, picking the thing up and staring at it.

"Press the button instead of fiddling with the damn thing!"

He looked startled at my tone, put it back on the table and turned it on.

*"Good morning there, Jim and Floyd. You guys are sure sound sleepers and I didn't want to wake you before I went out. You know, I'm beginning to think that this city is not for me. I need some space to get my thoughts together. I'm going to take a walk back down the wall, get some air to breathe, some space to think in. You hang in there and I'll be in touch."*

"That old Steengo," Floyd said. "What a character. That's

him all right. His voice, sure enough, and his way of thinking. Some guy!"

I looked up, looked him in the eye. His face was as grim as mine. He shook his head in a silent *no*. I did the same.

Steengo had not left that message. It was his voice all right. Easy enough for the electronic technicians to fake that.

Steengo was gone.

*What* had happened?

# CHAPTER 18

"I really slept," I said. "Like a rock. Thirsty."

"The same. I'll get some juice and a couple of glasses."

"Great idea."

I had scribbled the note by the time he came back, slipped it to him when I took the glass. He opened it behind the pitcher, read it.

*Place bugged. What do we do?*

He nodded as he passed me my glass of juice.

"Thanks," I said, watching him turn over the note and write on the back. I don't know if there were optical bugs as well as the audio ones. Until we found out we had to act as though there were. I kept the note in my palm when I read it.

*Steengo much concerned. Left these for you before we went to the show.*

I finished the juice, put my glass down, lifted my eyebrows quizzically. He pointed quickly at his closed fist. When he stood and passed me he dropped something small into my lap. I waited a minute before I poured more juice, drank it, sat back with my hand in my lap. Two small, soft objects. Familiar. I rubbed my nose and glanced at them.

Filter nose plugs. For neutralizing gas. Steengo had known something—or guessed something. He also knew how affected I had been by the sessions in the Veritorium. He had suspected that something physical, not just the training session itself, had gotten to me.

Of course! Obvious by hindsight. I knew of a dozen hypnotic gases that lowered the ability to think clearly, that left the brain open to outside influences. So it hadn't been emotion but plain old chemistry that had carried me away. Steengo had suspected this—but why hadn't he told me? Depressingly, I realized that the state of mind I had been in, probably caused by drugs in the earlier session, rendered that impossible. He knew he couldn't tell me. But had been suspicious enough to wear the plugs himself.

And when he saw me getting deeply involved in the ritual he had interrupted before it was too late, had brought the whole thing to a screeching halt. I felt my teeth grating together and forced myself to stop.

He had talked about mother and the key under her pillow —to these people who denied that women even existed!

With the realization of the enormity of his crime in the eyes of the Paradisians I felt a sudden overwhelming fear for his safety. Would they kill him—or worse—had they killed him already? They were certainly capable of anything, I was sure now of that.

What next? Communication with our backup team in the spacer above was very much in order. I had to get into the open, away from the bugs, and contact Tremearne. Bring him up to date. Something had happened to Steengo. And the rest of us surely were in danger as well—and Madonette, this might affect her. This entire affair was getting a nasty and dangerous edge to it.

And thinking about dangerous, there was the other *dangerous* always hanging over my head. My computer flashed me the highly unwelcome message of a flickering red nine. I had been asleep longer than I had realized.

Artifact or no I was just nine days away from my personal destiny. When I had first heard the thirty-day deadline on the poison I had not been too concerned. Thirty days is a lot of time. I thought.

Nine days was definitely not a lot of time at all. And with Steengo suddenly vanished I had more problems, not less.

"Going for a run," I called out to Floyd, leaping to my feet in a spasm of fear-sponsored energy. "Feel logy after all that sleep. Got to clear my head."

I slammed out the door and down the road even as he was answering. Taking a different route from my usual one—then changed direction at random. Up ahead was a field of polpet-tone trees, laid out in neat rows and bulging with fruit. I jogged into a path beside the trees, looking around as I ran. No one in sight. There was little chance the Paradisers would put bugs in among the trees.

But they could have. I turned into a freshly plowed field and ran between the furrows. I should be safe enough here. I clamped my jaw twice.

"Hello, Tremearne, are you there?"

*"Very much so, Jim. We have all been awaiting your report. Can you tell us what is happening—the recorder is running."*

I jogged in position for a bit, then bent to tie my shoe—then gave up and just sat on the ground while I finished the detailed report. I was tired; the chemicals still kicking around in my system had not been kind to me.

"That's it," I finished. "Steengo is gone. Might be dead . . ."

*"No. I can reassure you on that score. A few hours ago we had a radio message from him, just a few words, then contact was lost again. He must be somewhere deep in the city, behind walls the radio signals can't penetrate. He might have been moved from one site to another, was in the open long enough for a brief transmission."*

"What did he say?"

The recording was brief and scratchy. Beginning with static and dying in static. But it was pure Steengo all right.

*". . . never enough! When I get my fingers on you,*

*you . . ."* The next word was hard to make out—but I could think of a half dozen that filled the bill.

"What do you think we should do? Break out of here?"

*"No—go along with everything. You will be contacted."*

"Contacted? By whom, what, which? Come in, Tremearne."

There was no answer. I rose and brushed off my shorts. Very mysterious. Tremearne was up to something—but he was not talking about it. Must be worried about eavesdroppers. Maybe he knew something that I didn't.

I started back at a slow run, changed that to a fast walk. To a slow walk, then a crawl. If there had been any farther to go I would probably have done it on all fours. As it was I stumbled into our quarters and collapsed, gasping, onto the couch. Floyd looked astonished.

"You look like you've been dipped and rolled."

"I feel even worse than that. Water, quickly, lots of it!"

I drank until I was sloshing, then sipped a little bit more, handed the glass weakly back.

"Knocked myself out. Be a good buddy and get my pack. I got some vitamin pills there should pick me up." When he handed me the pack I clicked out a couple of Blast-offs, super-uppers, and swallowed one. "Vitamins, good for you," I said as I passed one over. Floyd was a little faster off the mental mark lately and did not ask any questions.

Our timing was pretty good. The wave of good feeling and energy was washing away my almost-terminal fatigue when Veldi threw open the door.

"On your feet!" he called out. I did not move.

"Veldi," I said. "Old and trusted servant. No soft knock? No sweet tones . . ."

"The word is out that you Stainless Steel Rats are just plain rats. Troublemakers. Just get going."

There was the quick thud-thud of marching feet and Sergeant Ljotur came in with an armed squad of soldiers. Armed with wicked-looking spears with gleaming points and barbed shafts.

"You are to come with me!" he ordered. He did not look happy about it.

"No longer a musical fan, Ljotur?" I said, climbing slowly to my feet.

"I have orders." Orders that he obviously did not like. Which of course he would obey since independent thought had never been encouraged in the military. Floyd followed me out and the squad formed up. Four in front, four in back of us. Ljotur checked the formation, nodded, took position in front and raised his spear.

"Forward—*burtu!*"

We burtu'ed at a slow trot, down the road and turned right at the corner. Which put us directly on the route to the red brick lodgings where Iron John lurked, as I remembered from our first visit. Trotted down the road and into a tunnel under a row of buildings. One of the guards to the rear tapped me on the shoulder.

"Give me a hand, will you?" he asked in a hoarse voice.

Then swung sideways and planted his fist in the stomach of the guard next to him. Who folded and dropped without a sound.

This was easy enough to understand. I had turned when he tapped me so I kept turning to face the rear. I reached out and got a hand on the other two guards' necks. Squeezed as they turned their spears towards me.

"Floyd!" I gasped out, putting all my energy into my throttle grips so these jokers would pass out before they harpooned me. "The others!"

One of the guards dropped but the other one, with a stronger neck, kept his spear coming. Into my stomach—

No, not quite. The first guard, who had called to me, gave him a quick chop under the ear. He and I whirled about, ready to jump to Floyd's help. And stopped.

The four other guards were lying in a silent, tumbled heap on the ground. Floyd had a spear pressed firmly under Ljotur's jaw, was holding him up with his other hand.

"You want to talk to this guy?" Floyd asked. "Or you want him down there with the others?"

"I've nothing to say . . ."

"No talk. Drop."

Before I could finish speaking a limp Ljotur joined the rest of the sleeping patrol.

"What about this one?" Floyd asked, fingers arced, pointing to the soldier who had called to me.

"Wait! He started this thing. There has to be a reason for it."

"There is," the soldier said in the same hoarse voice. "I am going to tell you a few things. You will not laugh at anything I say—understood?"

"We're not laughing!" I said. "Great, guy, thanks for the help. And what's the plan?"

"First off—remember about the laughing! I'm not a guy. I'm a girl. Do I see lips bending?"

"Never!" I called out, to disguise the fact that a little flicker of emotion *had* appeared. "You saved us. We are in your debt. We are not laughing. So tell us about it."

"All right. But let's drag these so-called soldiers out of the way first. Then we go on. The orders were to bring you to Iron John and that is what I am going to do. Your friend is in danger. Do nothing precipitate. Forward."

We went. Disbelieving perhaps, but still forward. Floyd started to talk but I raised my hand.

"Save the discussion. Explanations will be useful after we make sure Steengo is all right. But Floyd—stop me if I am wrong—did I see you take five guys out while I was just about managing two?"

"You didn't see it. It was over before you turned to look." He was the same old laid-back Floyd—but was that a new touch of firmness to his words? It was a day of surprises. And he was right—I had not seen him at work, just the results.

The brick palace jogged into view ahead. Apparently not all of the troops had been told that we were no longer heroes, for the guards at the entrance did a snappy jump to attention and salute as we trotted past.

"Halt!" our newfound friend (girl . . . ?) called out and we stopped before the guards at the door. "Orders to bring these two to Iron John. Permission to enter?"

"Enter!" the officer in charge called out. The doors opened and closed behind us as we trotted by. There was the large room ahead and inside it was Iron John. And just one other person.

Steengo. Collapsed against the wall, covered in bruises and blood. One eye swollen shut. He started to speak but could only rasp out something incomprehensible.

"You are all here now," Iron John said. "Soldier—guard the entrance. No one to enter or leave. I have a score to settle with these interlopers. Because I have changed my mind about keeping this thing quiet. I listened to my advisers and I am sorry that I did. Secrecy is at an end and justice will be done to the blasphemers. Here is what will happen. First I will kill this aged devil who spoke such filth. You two will watch.

"Then I will kill you as well."

He started towards Steengo, a red giant of unleashed power. Hands extended to kill.

# CHAPTER 19

"Let me have your spear." I called out to the soldier at the door. She shook her head in a silent *no,* then said, "I have my orders." No help from this source.

Iron John had turned and was walking towards Steengo. I ran two silent steps in his direction and launched myself into a flying kick to his back. Heel punching out, a killing blow.

Then I was batted from the air. As big as he was—Iron John was just as fast. He had turned while I was in the air and had swung one hand. Knocking me aside, sprawling me onto the floor. His voice was as deep and ominous as a distant volcano.

"Do you want to be first, little man? You wish the others to watch your destruction? Perhaps that is only fair since you are their leader."

He came slowly towards me and I found myself trembling with fear. Fear? Yes, because he was not human, more than human. He was Iron John a part of the legend of life, I could not hurt him.

*He wasn't!* I scrabbled to my feet, my leg ached, moved away. He was much bigger, wider, stronger than I was. But no, he wasn't a legend. He was a man.

"A big fat red slob!" I shouted. "A hairy conman!"

His eyes were wide, red, angry. His arched fingers reached for me. I feinted a fist at his jaw, saw him move to block it. Kept turning in an unstoppable kick to his knee.

It connected—but he made no attempt to avoid it. My foot hurt. His knee, his kneecap, looked unhurt.

"I am Iron John!" he shouted. "Iron—iron!"

I fell back, there was no escape. I swung a twisting punch that he took on his biceps. It felt like striking stone. Then his fist to my ribs sent me skidding down the room.

When I gasped in breath it hurt. Felt like something was broken there. Stand up, Jim! I got as far as my knees and he came on.

I blinked as I saw two arms encircle his legs, send him staggering. Kicking out. It was Steengo who had crawled behind him, tried to trip him. Who was now sent crashing back into the wall. To fall and not move again.

I was barely aware of this because the instant Iron John's attention had wandered I had jumped. Getting an arm around his neck, grappling my own wrist. Pulling my forearm tight against his throat to crush his larynx, to cut off blood and air. The armlock that kills in seconds. My face was buried in his rank red fur as I tightened hard, harder than I ever had before.

To no avail. I could feel the tendons in his neck stiffen like steel bars, taking the pressure that should have been on his throat. He lifted one hand slowly, then sank his fingers deep into my flesh—

—hurled me across the room to crash into the wall, fall.

I realized that the voice wailing in agony was my own. I could not move. The soldier at the door looked at me, looked away. Steengo had lain, motionless, since that single, terrible blow. Nor could I do much better myself, just able to crawl.

At least Iron John had felt my hold; he was rubbing at his neck. The smile had gone and frothed saliva now coated his lips. Death would be a single blow . . .

"Iron John—you have forgotten something. You have forgotten me."

Floyd was speaking. Thin, black-bearded, uninvolved. He

must have stood and watched while Steengo was stricken, I was felled. Only now did he move.

Quietly forward. Hands extended, fingers lightly bowed. Iron John was in a rage. Leaped and lashed out.

And missed because Floyd was not there. He was to one side, kicking the red giant in the ribs so that he stumbled and almost fell.

"Come here," Floyd said in a voice so low I could barely hear it. "Come and be destroyed."

Iron John was cautious now, knew how fast his new opponent could react. He opened his arms wide and came slowly forward. A force of nature. Implacable and inescapable.

Two quick thuds, two blows sounded and Iron John staggered. Floyd was out of his reach again, circling him slowly. A sudden kick, a blow, then away again.

Nothing Iron John did seemed to affect the outcome. He was wary, he attacked suddenly, reached out and struck. Touched only air. Floyd was before him, behind him—striking him. Wearing him down.

They circled for minutes this way. And Floyd was still just as fast, striking with impunity. But the red monster was going slower and slower, arms lower and lower as the endless blows drove the strength from them. He must have realized that there could be only one end to this battle, on these terms. But he was still dangerous. Almost by chance the struggle moved towards me.

He was after me I realized! I had only the shortest instant to draw my leg back before Iron John spun about and dived towards me.

And caught my kick full in his face. He dropped—but his hands closed on my ankle, pulled me towards him. Reached up . . .

Then Floyd struck. No science now—raw power. Pile driver blows to the giant's back and kidneys that opened his

mouth wide with pain, forcing him to release me as he struggled to get away from his tormentor.

More blows to his head. He tried to rise, his legs were
kicked from beneath him. The thudding of quick strikes like
some terrible machine at work. Then a sudden silence.

A moment for balance, no expression showing on his face,
then Floyd swung a terrible kick that terminated on the side of
the giant's head. Who fell over and did not rise nor move
again.

"Dead?" I croaked. Floyd knelt and felt the pulse in his
neck.

"No, he wasn't supposed to be. He'll survive. But I think
that he will remember he has been in a fight." He flashed a
quick smile, then his face became calm again. "If you're all
right I'll look at Steengo."

"I'm great. Knocked about but great," I croaked as I
climbed painfully to my feet.

"Pulse good," he said, kneeling beside our friend. "He has
taken a lot of punishment but nothing seems to be broken that
I can find. He will come out of this fine."

I was groggy, now even weaker with relief, blurted out the
words without thinking.

"He's fine. I'm fine. However we would have been a lot
better if you had waded into this fracas sooner."

I saw him wince at the words, wished I could take them
back. You never can.

"I'm sorry, I really am. I had to wait, see what he could do.
I know that you're good, Jim. I knew you could at least hold
him. I'm sorry but I had to see how fast he could move before
I took him on. I had to wear him down, not get touched. I
knew I could do it—and I moved as soon as I knew.
Sorry . . ."

"Reporting," our guard-guy-girl said. "The Red One is unconscious."

She lowered the small, coin-sized communicator as I stalked towards her, hands out and ready to strike.

"Who were you talking to? Whose side are you on? What's happening here? Speak—or get demolished."

The guard, spear lowered and pointed at me, stood her ground. "The answer to your questions is arriving now. There." The point of her spear moved to indicate a spot behind me. A ruse? Who knew, who cared. I turned and looked at Iron John's giant throne.

Which was slowly turning on some invisible axis. Floyd and I both faced that way, hands raised automatically on the defense. A black opening was revealed and, as the throne stopped moving, there was motion in the darkness beyond. Two figures appeared, walked out into the room.

Both women.

One of them was Madonette.

"Hi, guys," she said, smiling and waving. "I'd like to introduce a new friend, Mata."

The woman was about my height, regal of bearing in her dark robe touched with gold embroidery. Her expression was composed, peaceful; small wrinkles at the corners of her eyes, a touch of gray to her hair, were the only signs of age.

"Welcome to the other side of Paradise, Jim," she said—and held out her hand. Her handshake was firm and quick. I opened my mouth but could not think of anything relevant to say.

"I know that you have many questions." Her words filled the gap. "All of which will be answered. But it would be wisest to postpone our little chat until we are out of this place. A moment, please."

She took a very efficient-looking hypodermic from the reticule hanging at her waist. Uncapped it and bent to brush aside the thick hair on his leg to give Iron John a quick injection.

"He will sleep the better," she said. "Bethuel—will you lead the way?"

The guard raised her spear in a quick salute, then marched resolutely past the throne and into the opening. Madonette touched Steengo's cheek, then waved Floyd to her. "Help me carry him. Jim will have enough to do just moving himself."

I resented the remark—a blotch on my masculine pride?—but before I could stumble over they had lifted him and were following the guard, Bethuel.

There were no lights in the tunnel behind the throne. At least none until Mata had entered behind us and sealed it once again. Pale illumination flickered into existence. More than enough to see by. Nor was it a long walk to the open door at the far end. We emerged into a large, red brick room that could have been a mirror-image of the one that we had just left.

Just in physical size, though. Here the walls were covered by pleasant hangings, tapestries of sunshine and floral landscapes. Instead of the swords and shields that adorned the other. The stained-glass windows here depicted scenes of mountains and valleys, villages and forests. Unlike Iron John's windows which featured the clash of battle, spackle of gore. This was altogether more civilized.

As was the murmur of concerned voices from the women in attendance here. They tenderly carried Steengo to a couch where another woman, dressed in white, ministered to him. I dropped into the nearest chair and scowled around at all the female bustle. My voice, louder and more censorious than I had intended, cut through the peaceful scene.

"Now would somebody, anybody, tell me just what the hell is going on."

The way I was ignored was comment enough in itself. Though a smiling girl did bring me a glass of cool wine—on the way to serve the others. Madonette sat next to Mata, where they put their heads together for a moment before Madonette spoke.

"First—and most important now that you all are safe—is the fact that the artifact is here and is being looked after. In addition there is—"

"Excuse if I interrupt," I said. "A matter of priority." I clamped my jaw twice. "Did you hear that, Tremearne?" His answer buzzed in my jawbone.

"*I did, and . . .*"

"Priorities, Captain." I spoke quietly so only he could hear. "Mission complete. Alien artifact returned. Antidote for me on its way down. Nine days is close enough to come. Do you understand all that?"

"*Of course. But there is a complication . . .*"

"Complication!" I could hear the squeak of fear edging my voice. "What?"

"*I sent for the antidote to the thirty-day poison as soon as I heard about it. I had no intention of waiting until the deadline to administer it. However there was an accident in transit.*" Sweat suddenly beaded my forehead and my toes tapped anxiously on the floor. "*These things happen. I've sent for a second batch and it's en route now.*"

I cursed viciously under my breath, then realized that I was the object of more than one concerned glance. Smiled woodenly and snarled my answer.

"Do it. Get it. No excuses. *Now.* Understood."

"*Understood.*"

"Fine." I stopped whispering and called out. "I'm most cheered to hear that the artifact has been found. Now, if you please, an explanation of what all this is about."

"Seems obvious," Madonette said undoubtedly miffed by my surly behavior. "It looks like the ladies have saved your bacon and you should be grateful."

Which did nothing to clear the air. "As I recall," I recalled. "It was the gentlemen—at some physical cost I must add—who polished off that russet rottweiler before you all came onto the scene. I also remember that we were watched all the time during the life-and-death struggle by one of your lot who did nothing to help."

The tough answer sprang to her lips and I snarled around at the female company. Tempers flared on all sides but Mata cooled things down.

"Children—there has been enough tribulation and pain, so do not cause yourself any more." She turned to me. "Jim, let me explain. The soldier who aided your escape, Bethuel, is one of our spies who keeps us informed about all the masculine meanderings beyond the wall. I ordered her to help you escape your guards, which she did. I also ordered her not to reveal her presence to Iron John. The men beyond the wall have no idea that we watch them closely and I wish it to remain that way. She aided your escape and you should be grateful."

I was, and I should have admitted it, but I was still bullheaded and angry and settled for a surly mutter and growl. Mata nodded blithely as though I had communicated something of importance.

"See how well everything has worked out? You are here and safe, your friends safe as well, and that for which you seek, the strange artifact, is secure and close by."

I only half listened. Fine for the troops. But there were other forces at work that did not bode well for my future. Accidents in transit did not happen by accident. Someone in the bureaucracy that was manipulating me—did not like me. Perhaps had never liked me and never had any intention of supplying the antidote. I would certainly be less trouble to them if I were safely dead. And there were only nine days left to sort the whole thing out.

I had touched my computer controls automatically while these thoughts were whizzing about my tired brain. The number glowed before me. I really had had a longer sleep than I realized.

Eight days to go.

# CHAPTER 20

I looked around at the peaceful female bustle—and suddenly felt very, very tired. My side hurt and I felt sure that a couple of ribs were broken. I sipped the wine but it didn't help. What I really needed was a couple of Blast-off pills to restore me to something resembling life. In my pack—

"My pack!" I shouted hoarsely. "My equipment, everything. Those masculine momsers have all our gear!"

"Not quite," Mata said in soothing tones. "As soon as you left we saw to it that the porter, Veldi, was rendered unconscious and both your packs are here now. Your associate Steengo's equipment was not in your residence so we can assume that it is now in the possession of Iron John or his associates."

"Not good." I worried a fingernail with my incisors. "There are things there they shouldn't see . . ."

"*Might I interrupt,*" Tremearne's voice spoke through my jaw-a-phone. "*I was waiting until things quieted down to tell you. Steengo's pack is safe.*"

"You have it?"

"*Rather I should have said 'made safe.' All of your packs are booby-trapped with a canister of rotgrot. Which, when released by a coded radio signal, causes the contents of the pack to instantly decay to their component molecules.*"

"Nice to know. A lot of secrets are being revealed of late, aren't they?"

There was no response from my jaw. I held out my wineglass for a refill. "Some simple answers to some simple questions, if you please." My anger had been blasted by fatigue, excoriated by fear of imminent death. Mata nodded in response.

"Good. On a historical note—how come guys over there, girls here?"

"A union of convenience," Mata said. "Many years ago our foremothers were forcefully relocated to this planet. This inadvertent transplantation had a sobering effect on them. Whatever excesses of zeal they had displayed on other worlds were not repeated here. Peace, cool-reasoning and logic prevailed. We became then as you see us now."

"Women," I said. "A society of women."

"That is correct. Life here was a running battle for a good long time, or so it is written. The Fundamentaloids tried to convert us, while our next door neighbors tried to wipe us out. The inferior sex they called us, a threat to their existence. When we first came to this planet we found that those macho crazies were already well established. Our group was forced to spend a good deal of effort just staying clear of them. This was time and energy wasted, our founding mothers decided, so they sought for ways to bring about peace. Eventually they convinced the male ruling clique that they could prosper by utilizing their energy in a more positive manner. It was a completely selfish appeal, arranging ways for the males on top in their society to stay on top, while providing absolute control of the rest of the men."

"Sounds pretty terrible," Madonette said. "Turning all those men into slaves."

"Never say slaves! Willing collaborators is more like it. We showed those in charge, and in particular the one now called Iron John, how much easier it would be to rule by brain rather than muscle. We demonstrated to their satisfaction how a great deal more could be accomplished. With our intelligence and knowledge of science, and their muscles, two separate societies were born. In the beginning there was much hatred and clashes between the groups. This died away when it was decided that only the male leaders knew of our existence. This suited the leaders to perfection."

"That was when the two cities were built—and the wall?"

"Correct. This planet is rich in red clay and fossil fuel so the males soon became manic brick makers. After we showed them how to build kilns, of course. There were contests to see who could mold the most bricks, or fire the greatest number, or carry the most. The champion was named brickie of the month and achieved great renown. This went on until you couldn't see the trees for the mountains of bricks. We quickly researched brick laying in our data bases and put the men to work on that."

She sipped her wine delicately and waved her hand in a circle. "Here are the results—and quite attractive they are too. While our physical scientists were sorting the males out this way, our cultural engineers were looking at the sloppy mucho-macho theories that had been keeping them going up to this point. The Iron Hans myth was only a part of their pantheon. We simplified and altered it. Then used genetic biology to modify the physical structure of their leader, so he is as you see him now. At first he was grateful, although gratitude has long since vanished."

"How long?"

"Hundreds of years. Cellular longevity was part of the treatment."

I was beginning to catch on. "And I'll bet that you remember this firsthand—since you and the other lady leaders have had the same treatments?"

She nodded, pleased. "Very adroit, James. Yes, the authorities on both sides of the wall have had the treatments. This makes for continuity of leadership—"

"And the need for secrecy of each other's existence that keeps the powerful in power?"

Mata shook her head in wonder. "You are indeed most perspicacious. How I wish you were in charge next door rather than that hairy halfwit."

"Thanks for the job offer—but no thanks. So the men beyond the wall don't know that you women are here. The same must be true of your women—"

"Not at all. They know about the males—and just don't care. We have a complete and satisfactory society. Childbearing for those who wish it, a fulfilling intellectual life for all."

"And religion? Do you have a female equivalent of Iron John?"

She laughed merrily at the thought, as did all the other women who were listening to our conversation. Even Madonette was smiling until she saw my glare, turned away.

"That's it," I snapped. "Enjoy yourself. And when you are through, if you ever are, you might kindly let me know the joke."

"I am sorry, James," Mata said, laughter gone and really quite serious. "We were being rude and I apologize. The answer to your question is a simple one. Women don't need myths to justify their femininity. All of the myths about Iron Hans, Iron John, Barbarossa, Merlin and other mythological men with their salvation myths are all purely male. Just think about it. I am not making a value judgment, just an observation. Such as the observation that men are basically combative, confrontational, insecure and unstable—and appear to need these myths to justify their existence."

There was a lot to argue with there, maybe not a lot but some. A good deal of jumping-to-conclusions and more than a bit of rationalization. I sidestepped for the moment, until I knew more about how this society ticked. I raised a finger.

"Now let me see if I have this straight. You ladies have a comfortable existence on this side of the wall. You provide the scientific backup to the males on the other side. To keep them chuntering along in their locker-room paradise. Correct?"

"Among other things. That is basically correct."

"Dare I ask what they supply in return?"

"Very little, if the truth be known. Fresh meat from the nomads. Who not only won't trade with us but now heartily deny our existence, though they secretly would love to wipe us out. Then there is an occasional supply of sperm to top up our cryogenic sperm bank. Little else. We watch them and keep them going mostly by habit—and for our own safety. If the man in the street doesn't know that we exist he can't cause us any trouble. The men also get a lot of pleasure in bashing the nomads when they start bothering us. Altogether a satisfactory relationship."

"It certainly sounds that way." I finished the glass of wine and realized that I was beginning to feel the effects of the alcohol. Which was better than feeling the bruises and sore ribs. Which should be looked at soon—but not too soon. The unfolding drama of cultural mish-mash was just too interesting. "If you please—a question or two before we call in the medics. First is the most important question. You mention sperm banks so I assume that pregnancy and motherhood still exist?"

"They certainly do! We would never consider depriving women of their hormonal, psychological and physical rights. Those who wish to become mothers become mothers. Simple enough."

"Indeed it is. And looking around I see that they are lucky enough to all have female babies."

For the first time I saw Mata less than completely relaxed and calm. She looked away, looked back—took up her glass and sipped some more wine.

"You must be tired," she finally said. "We can finish this discussion some other time . . ."

"Mata!" Madonette gasped. "I think that you are avoiding

the topic. This cannot be. I have so admired you and your people here. You are not going to tell me that I am wrong?"

"No, never!" Mata said reaching out and taking Madonette's hands in hers. "It has just been so long since we discussed these things. Decisions were taken that seemed excellent at the time. Some of us have had reservations since, but, well nothing much can really be done at this point . . ."

Her voice ran down and she emptied her wineglass. She was upset and I felt sorry for pinning her down like that. I yawned.

"You're right," I said. "I think rest and recuperation come first."

Mata shook her head in a firm *no.* "Madonette is right. These decisions must be faced, discussed. Approximately half of the pregnancies are male, male fetuses. This is determined in the first few weeks." She saw Madonette's worried expression and shook her head again.

"No—please hear me out and don't think the worst. All healthy pregnancies are brought to term. In the case of the males the bottle banks are used—"

"Bottle banks! Isn't that an unfortunate term?"

"Perhaps in your society, Jim. But here it simply signifies highly perfected artificial wombs. Technically superior if truth be known. There are no spontaneous miscarriages, no effects of bad diet and so forth. And at the end of nine months the healthy male babies are—"

"Decanted?"

"No, born. As soon as they are viable the men take over. Specially trained nursemen who supervise the healthy growth of the boys. Their education and assimilation into their society."

"Very interesting," I said, for it certainly was. I hesitated about the next question, but curiosity was gnawing away and could not be suppressed. "Even more interesting is where do the men think the babies come from?"

"Why don't you ask them?" Mata said coldly and I realized that this interview was at an end.

"Now I really am tired—to be continued," I breathed, dropping back into the couch. "Is there a doctor in the house?"

This kicked a lot of maternal instinct into gear and extracted a great deal of attention. I didn't feel the injection that knocked me out. Or the one that brought me to much later. The women were gone and we were alone. Madonette was holding my hand. Which she dropped with slow deliberation when she saw that my eyes were open.

"The good news, stalwart Jim, is that none of your bones are broken. Just a lot of bruising. Better news is that the treatment for the bruises is under way. Best news is that Steengo is in pretty good shape, all things considered, and wants to see you."

"Bring him in."

"In a moment. While you were sleeping I talked to Mata. She told me a lot more about how things work around here."

"Did you find out about the babies?"

"She really is a nice person, Jim. Everyone here has been very nice to me and . . ."

"But you are beginning to have some reservations?"

She nodded. "More than a few. Things look so nice on the surface—and maybe they are. But it is the babies that bother me. I am sure that they are well taken care of physically, even mentally. But to believe a stupid myth!"

"Which one of the stupid myths going about is the one that bothers you?"

"Spontaneous creation would you believe! All the males gather around Iron John's pool for a ceremony of life. The golden balls drift up through the water and are seized. And each one contains a healthy happy baby! And grown men believe that nonsense!"

"Grown men—and women—have believed worse nonsense down through the ages. This myth was a common one for the so-called lower forms of life. Flies being spontaneously created in manure heaps. Because no one bothered making the connection between grubs growing there and flies laying eggs. All of the creation myths of mankind, all the gods dropping down and molding clay and breathing life, the virgin births and the like. They are all nonsense once they are examined. But we have to start somewhere I suppose. I'm just not happy where some of these people are ending up."

There was a rattle and a thump as the door was opened. Floyd pushed in the wheelchair and Steengo lifted a white-wrapped hand.

"Looks like you did it, Jim. End of mission. Congratulations."

"And the same to you—and Floyd. And since it is The Stainless Steel Rats together, perhaps for the last time, would you mind making a few things clear. I have long felt that there was more than random chance in your selection. Dare I ask— just who are you three people? I suspect that you were chosen for more than musical ability—right Steengo?"

He nodded his bandaged head. "Almost right. Madonette is just what she appears to be . . ."

"Just an office drudge—singing for a hobby."

"The office's loss is music's gain." I smiled and blew a kiss her way. "One down, two to go. Steengo, I have a feeling that you really aren't retired. Right?"

"Right. And I do take some pride in my musical abilities. Which, if you must know, was why I was suckered into this operation by my old drinking buddy, Admiral Benbow."

"*Drinking buddy!* He who drinks with an admiral . . ."

"Must be an admiral too. Perfectly correct. I am Arseculint . . ."

"I didn't quite catch that."

"Arseculint is an acronym for Area Sector Commander Cultural Intercourse. And you can uncurl your lip. Perhaps, in context, 'intercourse' is not quite the right word. Cultural Relationships might express it better. My degrees are in archeology and cultural anthropology, which is what attracted me to the civil service in the first place. Sort of hands-on application of theory. I followed the matter of the alien artifact with a great deal of interest. So I was ripe for the plucking, you might say, when Stinky Benbow asked me to volunteer."

"Stinky?"

"Yes, funny nickname, goes back to the academy, something to do with a chemistry experiment. Which is completely beside the point. I thought enough of this assignment to take a leave from my desk. Great fun. Up until the last, that is."

"Which leaves young Floyd here? Also an admiral?"

He looked sheepish. "Come on, Jim, you know better than that. I even washed out of college, never graduated at all . . ."

I pointed an accusatory finger. "Putting academic credits aside you must have some value to the Special Corps."

"Yes, well, I do. I really am sort of an instructor . . ."

"Speak up, Floyd," Steengo said proudly. "Being chief instructor in charge of the unarmed defense school is nothing to be ashamed of."

"I agree completely!" I said. "If you weren't a whiz kid in unarmed combat, why none of us would be here. Thanks guys. Mission complete and successful. Let's drink to that."

As we raised and clashed our glasses together, drank deep, I thought of my mother. I do this very rarely; it must be all the male-female myth dredging that brought her to mind. Or what she used to say. Very superstitious my Ma. Had a superstition for any occasion. The one that I remember best was when you said how great things were, or what a nice day it was. *Bite your tongue* she used to say.

Meaning don't tempt the gods. Keep your head down. Because saying that something was good would surely bring about the opposite.

Bite your tongue, good old Ma. What a lot of malarky.

When I lowered my glass I saw a woman stumble in through the open door. A young woman with torn clothing, dusty and staggering.

"Sound the alarm . . ." she gasped. "Disaster . . . destruction!"

Madonette caught her as she fell, listened to her whispered words, looked up with a horrified expression.

"She's hurt, babbling . . . something about . . . the science building, destroyed, gone. Everything."

That was when I felt the cold tongs grab tight to my chest, squeezing so hard they made speech almost impossible.

"The artifact—" was all I managed to say.

Madonette nodded slow agreement. "That's where it was, they told me. In the science building. So it must be gone too."

# CHAPTER 21

The mutual decision of The Stainless Steel Rats was a simple one: we had had about enough for one day. We were alive, if not too well. We had found the artifact so our mission was accomplished. The fact that it had also been destroyed was beside the fact. I hoped. They would have to supply me with the poison antidote now. I kept that thought firmly before me as I went to sleep. This was a time for rest. Wounds had to heal, tissue had to mend, fatigue had to be alleviated: medication and a good night's sleep took care of all of that.

The sun was shining brilliantly upon the garden of our new residence when I dragged myself there next morning. Sleep had banished fatigue, which meant that I felt all the bruises that much more enthusiastically. My medication was beginning to override the pain and I dropped into a chair while I waited for beneficence to take place. Steengo came in soon after, swinging along on crutches and looking very much like I felt. He eased himself into the chair opposite me. I smiled a welcoming smile.

"Good morning, Admiral."

"Please, Jim—I'm still Steengo."

"Then, Steengo, since we're alone for the moment, let me express my heartfelt thanks for breaking up the brainwashing session with Iron John. For which, unhappily, you paid quite a physical price."

"Thank you, Jim, I appreciate that. But I had to do it. To save you from being programmed. Also—I really did lose my temper. Teddy bear indeed! A complete corruption of history."

"No teddy bear? No golden ball?"

"The golden ball, yes. That represents innocence, the pleasures of childhood without responsibility. It is lost when we grow up. To regain this freedom the myth tells us we have to find the ball under mother's pillow—and steal it."

"But in a society without women you can't have a mother —so the myth has to be rewritten?"

Steengo nodded agreement, then winced and touched the bandage around his head. "Retold as nonsense. In the original story Mother never wants the boy child to grow up, sees him as young and dependent forever. Independence must be stolen away from mother—hence the golden ball under her pillow."

"Pretty deep stuff."

"Pretty fascinating stuff. Mankind depends on its myths to rationalize existence. Pervert the myth and you pervert society."

"Like Big Red and his mates on the other side of the wall?"

"Exactly. But what was happening there was far more dangerous than just editing a myth. I had suspected that there would be some strong narcogases in the air—and I was right. You and Floyd were glassy-eyed and practically hypnotized into immobility. So it wasn't just a matter of listening to one more story about the magnetic field of the deep masculine. This was about having a very pernicious and demented theory punched deep into your mind, into your subconscious. You were being brainwashed, thought-controlled—and this sort of crude forced suggestion can do infinite harm. I had to stop it."

"Risking your own life at the same time?"

"Perhaps. But I am sure you would have done the same for me if the circumstances were reversed."

There was no answering that one. Would I? I smiled, a little grimly. "Can I at least say thanks?"

"You can. Greatly appreciated. So back to work. Now, before the others come, to more pressing business. Since I am now in the open, so to speak, I am relieving Captain Tremearne and taking command of this operation. I am in a better position to kick the cagal out of the chain of command and make sure that your antidote is here instantly. Or sooner. My first imperative order when I took command was to send for it."

"Then you know about the thirty-day poison? If I might be frank—I can tell you—it has had me pretty worried. Thank you—"

"Don't thank me yet. Because I want your assurance that you will stick with this assignment, thirty-day poison or no."

"Of course I will. I took on this job, got paid, and gave my word I would finish it. The poison was just some bureaucratic moron's idea of a completion bond."

"I was sure you would say that. Knew that you would carry on regardless, threat of death or no threat of death."

Why was I uncomfortable when he said this? This was my old mate Steengo talking. Or was there a strong whiff of the admiral behind his words? Once the military, always the military . . . No, I would not think ill of him. But I better remember that the poison was still churning away. He was smiling widely and I let my smile mirror his. Although, deep inside, the worry and fear still nagged and scratched at my thoughts. Find the artifact, Jim. That is the only way to be sure about the antidote.

I laughed and smiled. But only on the outside. "Carry on, of course. The artifact must be found."

"Must be found, you are right. The search must go on!" He looked over my shoulder and waved. "And there's Floyd— and Madonette. Welcome, my dear, welcome. I would stand to greet you, but only with difficulty."

She smiled and kissed his forehead below the bandage. Of course she was the last one to arrive, woman's prerogative. Though I had better abandon such male-chauv-pig reflexive observations. At least while I was still a guest of the ladies this side of Paradise.

"I have been talking to Mata," she said, seating herself and sipping a bit of fruit juice. "The science building was empty when the explosion occurred, so no one was injured. Since then they have sifted the ruins and found that there is no trace at all of the artifact."

"Positive?" I asked.

"Positive. They have been eavesdropping on the other side of the wall, so they knew about all our interest in the thing. They waited until they observed that all the male scientists had looked at it and prodded it enough. As expected those noble gentlemen—referred here to as 'the geriatric incompetents'— had discovered nothing. Having no further interest the scientists had it transferred here. A study program had been drawn up to examine the artifact but was just beginning when the explosion occurred. End of report."

So the artifact might have been stolen, might still be around. I could help look for it. But I could also stop counting the days. Earlier, when I had been woken up by my computer, it had been flashing a glowing seven for my benefit. Now Admiral Steengo had relieved me of this chronic worry.

But I had taken three million for this job—and I still wondered what the thing really was. So the artifact-chase would continue. Minus the pressure of the days. I looked around at my musical rats and realized that nothing had changed for them. The search for the artifact was still on. Well—why not!

"What do we do next?" I said. Steengo, now more of an admiral than a musician, toted up the possible options.

"Was the explosion an accident? If it wasn't—who caused it? There are really a lot of questions that must be asked . . ."

"Mata told me to tell you that you were to ask Aida if you had any questions," Madonette said brightly.

We considered this seriously for a moment, then realized we hadn't the slightest idea of what she was talking about. Still the admiral, Steengo spoke for all of us.

"Who is Aida?"

"Not who—but what. An acronym for Artificially Intelligent Data Assembler. I think that it is the central computer here. In any case, here is the access terminal."

She put what looked like an ordinary portaphone on the table and switched it on. Nothing happened.

"Are you there, Aida?" Madonette said.

"Ready to be summoned at *any* time, darling," the voice said. In a rich and sexy contralto.

"I thought you said computer?" was my baffled response.

"Do I hear a male voice?" Aida said. Then giggled. "It has been such a *very* long time! Might I ask your name, sweetie?"

"Jim—not sweetie. And why did you call me *that*?"

"Training and programming, dear boy. Before this present assignment I ran an exploration spacer. Male crew, *endless* years in space. It was felt by my creators that a female voice and presence would be more efficacious morale-wise than a machine or masculine presence."

"The last exploration spacer was junked centuries ago," Steengo said.

"A lady does *not* like to be reminded of her age," Aida said huskily. "But it is true. When my ship was sent to the breakers I was made redundant. Since I am basically a computer program I am—every woman's dream—eternal. I had, shall we say, a rather varied career before I ended up here. Mind you, I'm not complaining. I find this *such* a pleasant occupation. There are charming ladies to talk to, as well as additional memory banks and data bases to access whenever I wish to. Most pleasurable—but I do chatter on. I have been

informed that you have a problem. If you would identify yourselves by name it would make conversation that much easier.
Jim and Madonette I know. The name of the gentleman who
just spoke?"

"Admiral—" Steengo said, then broke off.

"Let us *do* keep it on a first-name basis. And your first
name is Admiral. Others?"

"Floyd," said Floyd.

"And a great pleasure to meet you all. How may I help?"

"An item, referred to as the artifact, was recently brought
to the science building. Do you know about it?"

"Indeed I do. I was studying it, so am therefore quite familiar with the strange construction. In fact I had it under
observation at the time of the explosion."

"Did you see what happened to it?"

"Taking the literal meaning of *see,* dear Jim, forces me to
answer that question in the negative. I had no photo pickups
operating at the time so I did not physically see what happened to it. The only information I had was the direction that
it left in. That was thirty-two degrees to the right of the zero
north-polar latitude."

"There is nothing at all out there in that direction,"
Steengo said. "No settlements, no nomadic tribes. Nothing but
empty plains right up the polar cap. How do you know that
the artifact was taken that way?"

"I know that, *mon Amiral,* because this artifact emits
tachyons and I was observing it with a tachyometer. Keeping
count, so to speak, and most interesting it was too. It did not
emit many—after all, *what* source does?—but a few are much
better than none. Let the record show that it emitted one
tachyon, from the direction I have given you, just microsec-
onds before the explosion that destroyed the equipment I was
using."

"You weren't—injured?" Madonette said.

"How sweet of you to ask! I wasn't, because I wasn't there. As soon as I could I constructed a new tachyometer, conveyed it to the site of the explosion with, unhappily, no results. Now there is just background radiation."

"Do you know what caused the explosion?"

"Welcome to this easy give-and-take of social intercourse, friend Floyd. To answer your question—I do. It was a very powerful explosive. I can give you the chemical formula but I am sure that you would find that immensely boring. But I can tell you that this explosive was manufactured quite widely for the mining industry at one time. It is named ausbrechitite."

"Never heard of it."

"Understandable, Admiral, since it was found to grow unstable with the passage of time. Manufacturing was phased out and ausbrechitite was replaced by newer and more stable explosives."

"When was this?" I asked.

"A bit over three centuries ago. Would you like the exact date?"

"That will do fine."

We blinked at each other in silence. Not knowing what to do with this weird historical-scientific evidence. Only Madonette had the brains to ask the right question.

"Aida—do you have any theories about what happened?"

"Simply *thousands* my dear. But there is no point in telling you about them until I gather some more evidence. Right now you might say that we are in the early moves of a chess game with millions of possibilities for the rest of the game. But I can give you some figures. Chances of an accidental explosion; zero. Chances that the explosion was tied in with the theft; sixty-seven percent. What happens next depends upon you."

"How?"

"Consider reality. You are mobile, *cher* Jim while I am, so to speak, tied down to the job. I can give advice, and accompany you in transceiver form when you leave here. But what happens next—that decision is up to you."

"What decision?" Aida could be exasperating at times.

"I will supply a new tachyometer. If you take it in the direction I have indicated you might be able to track the artifact in this manner."

"Thanks," I said and reached out and turned Aida off. "Looks like us humans have to come to a decision. Who follows the trail? Let us not all speak at once but let me speak first because I am top rat. I have the feeling that it is now time to thin our ranks. I say that Madonette does not go any further. We needed her for the music—and wonderful she was too!—but not for crawling around looking for nutcases planting century-old bombs."

"I second Jim's motion," Admiral Steengo said.

"I third it," Floyd said quickly as Madonette tried to speak. "This is really not your kind of job. Nor is it Steengo's either."

"Isn't that for me to decide?" Steengo snarled in his best admiralish mode.

"No," I suggested. "If you wish to be of assistance, you can really help us by organizing the base operation from here. I declare that the motion has been seconded and passed above all objections. This is only a democracy when it suits me."

Steengo smiled and the admiral's scowl vanished; he was too smart to argue. "I agree. I am well past my sell-by date for fieldwork. My aching bones tell me that. Please, Madonette, give in graciously to the thrust of history. Are you nodding—albeit reluctantly? Good. Above and beyond any aid given by Aida, I will see to it that the Special Corps will supply any equipment needed. Questions?" He glowered around in a circle but we were silent. He nodded with satisfaction and Madonette raised her hand.

"With that decision out of the way—may I pass on a request? In conversation I have discovered that everyone here is a true musical Rat fan so . . ."

"Could we do one last gig before the group breaks up? You betcha. All in agreement."

There was a rousing cheer from all except Steengo who looked unhappy at the thought of all of his instruments reduced to a pile of particles. But Madonette, ever resourceful, had done a bit of work before she mentioned the gig.

"I've asked around among the girls. They tell me that there is a really nice chamber group here, as well as a symphony orchestra—they must have at least one instrument Steengo can play."

"Any of them, all of them—just unleash me!" he said and now it was smiles and cheers all around.

Due to the miracles of modern medicines, curing and healing drugs, pain-killers and a large shot of booze for Steengo, we were ready to do our performance later this same day. A matinee, since night here was still a couple of our days away and not worth waiting for.

There was quite a turnout at the sports stadium. Cheers and shouts of joy greeted us and no one seemed to mind that Steengo was not only out of costume but playing from a wheelchair. If this was to be the last curtain for The Stainless Steel Rats we meant to make it a performance to remember. Leaving the more militaristic and macho songs aside for the moment we launched into a mellow blues number.

> *Blue world—*
> *Hear me singing my song.*
> *Blue world—*
> *What's it I done wrong?*
> *Blue world—*
> *You gonna help me along*
> *Blue wor-r-r-ld.*

*Here we are—*
*We ain't goin' away.*
*Here we are—*
*On this planet to stay.*
*Blue wor-r-r-ld.*

*Landing was easy,*
*Plenty of fun.*
*Down came our rocket—*
*'Neath the blue sun.*
*Landing was great—*
*Everything swell.*
*Now it's all over,*
*Living is hell,*
*Down here at the bottom of the gravity well.*

We did many an encore this day. Finished finally with the feeling of exhaustion and happiness that only comes with an artistic job well done. Sleep came easily but, unable to resist, I took one last peek at the days remaining before closing my eyes.

Still seven. Still a week. Plenty of time for my good buddy Admiral Steengo to kick butt and come up with the antidote. I think I was smiling when I closed my eyes which, when you think about it, was quite a change from the preceding twenty-seven days. Yes it was.

Then why wasn't I going to sleep? Instead of lying there tensely staring into the darkness. An easy answer.

Until the happy moment when I pulled back the plunger and shot up with the antidote I had only seven days to live.

Nighty-night, Jim. Sleep well . . .

# CHAPTER 22

Either I was a slugabed or the admiral, released from his role as a musician, was a workaholic. Or both. Because by the time I had appeared he had single-handedly organized our expedition down to the last detail. He was muttering over the heap of apparatus as he punched the checklist into his handheld. He glanced up, waved vaguely, then finished off the last items.

"This is your new backpack. It contains a number of items you will probably need—and here's a printout of what's inside it. I assume that you have a good deal of illegal and possibly deadly items in your old pack which you can transfer after I leave. Aida is assembling another tachyometer and I'm going to get it now. Floyd will join you shortly—and here is Madonette, welcome, welcome."

Steengo made as graceful an exit as he could on crutches. Madonette, a picture of good cheer, swept in and took both of my hands in hers. Then discovered that this wasn't an enthusiastic enough greeting so she kissed me warmly on my cheek. My arms embraced her in automatic response, but closed on empty air since she had already whirled away and dropped onto the couch.

"I wish that I were coming with you, Jim—but I know that it's impossible. Still, I'm not looking forward to getting back to the stuffy old office."

"I'm going to miss you," I said. Meaning it to be a calm

statement but listening to myself in horror as it came out all dewy-eyed and smarmy. "All of us will miss you, of course."

"Same here. There were some hairy moments—but you took care of everything, didn't you?" The warmth and appreciation were such that I could feel myself blushing. "All in all I think it was an experience of a lifetime. And I am definitely not going back to all those files and staff meetings and sealed windows. It's field work from now on. Out in the fresh air! Isn't that a good idea?"

"Wonderful, yes indeed," I said, missing her already. I don't know where all this might have ended if Floyd hadn't made a disgustingly cheerful entrance.

"Morning all. Good day for the expedition. Hi and unhappily good-by Madonette, companion of many an adventure. It has been fun working with you."

"Could you teach me unarmed defense?"

"My pleasure. Easy enough if you work at it."

"Then I could train to be a field agent?"

"Probably not. But I'll sure look into it."

"Would you! I'd be ever grateful. I was telling Jim that I don't want to work in an office anymore."

"Nor should you! A girl with your talents can find much better occupation."

They smiled at each other from opposite ends of the couch, knees almost touching, wrapped up in each other. I was forgotten. I hated Floyd's guts. Was more than happy to hear the thud of crutches and the dragging footsteps approaching.

"All here," Steengo said. "Very good. The tachyometer is ready."

The thing that was following him now trotted forward. Walking, stiff-legged, was the ugliest fake dog that I had ever seen in my life. It was covered in black artificial fur with handfuls missing, had beady black eyes like buttons, stuck out a dry red tongue as it barked.

"Bow-wow."

"What do you mean 'bow-wow'?" I gasped aloud. "What is this repulsive object?"

"The tachyometer," Admiral Steengo said.

"Bow-wow," it barked again. "And for convenience sake the tachyometer is mounted within this mobile terminal."

"Aida?" I said.

"None other. Do you like this disguise?"

"I have never seen a more artificial artificial dog in my life!"

"Well don't get *too* insulting about it. Fido is state of the art—and that is *modern* art if you are thinking something nasty. For one thing the dear little doggy communicates with me by gravimetric waves which, as I am sure you know, cannot be blocked like radio waves. They penetrate the most solid buildings, cut through the most gigantic mountain ranges. So we are always in communication, always in touch. Admittedly Fido here has seen better days. But you know what they say about beggars?"

"I do. But we're choosers without being beggars and I choose a better mobile terminal."

"Your choice, handsome. Give me two days and you can have whatever you want."

Two days? And I had like maybe six and a half to live unless the antidote arrived. I took a deep breath and whistled.

"Here Fido. Nice doggie. Let's go walkies."

"Bow-wow," it said and began to pant most artificially.

"This is the plan," Admiral Steengo said. "I will monitor this operation from the orbiting spacer along with Captain Tremearne. Jim and Floyd will head north in the direction taken by the missing artifact. Aida will be in contact with this terminal, that will also be searching for a tachyon emission source." He appeared to run out of words and rubbed his jaw.

"A nice plan," I said, but I could not keep a certain tone

of derision out of my voice. "Cooked down to essentials it means that we just trot north until something happens."

"A satisfactory interpretation. Good luck."

"Thanks. And you will keep the other and most pressing matter of a certain injection on the top of your agenda?"

"I shall query the people involved hourly on the hour," he said grimly—and I think he meant it.

We filled our packs, kept the good-bys as brief as possible, loaded up and followed Fido out without a backward glance. I liked Madonette. Perhaps too much while I was on an assignment like this. Go, Jim, go I cozened. Follow your wandering tachyon.

We followed the flapping black nylon tail through the streets and onward to the outlying farms. The women we met waved happily, some even whistling bits of our tunes to cheer us on the way. The last farm fell behind us and the open plains opened out ahead. I clacked my jaw-radio.

"Are you there, Tremearne?"

*"Listening in."*

"Any tribes of nomads around—or up ahead?"

*"Negative."*

"Any buildings, farms, people, sheots—anything visible on this heading?"

*"Negative. We've done a detailed scan as far north as the polar ice. Nothing."*

"Thanks. Over and out." Wonderful.

"Empty on all sides, nothing at all ahead," I reported to Floyd. "So we just stay on this heading until our plastic retriever detects any tachyons—or we reach the north pole and freeze to death."

"I've been meaning to ask. What's a tachyon?"

"Good question. Up until now I thought it was just a theoretical unit that the physicists dreamed up in order to explain how the universe works. One of the subatomic entities that exist either as waves or particles. Until they are observed they

have no real existence. It has been said, and who am I to
doubt it, that they exist in a probabilities limbo of many possible superimposed states." I noticed that Floyd's jaw was beginning to drop, his eyes to glaze. He shook his head.

"You are going to have to try harder, Jim—you lost me a
long time back."

"Right, sorry. Try this. There are various kinds of units in
physics. A photon is a unit of light energy and an electron is a
unit of electric energy. Okay?"

"Great. With you so far."

"A graviton is a unit of gravity and a tachyon a unit of
time."

"Lost me again. I thought minutes and seconds were units
of time?"

"They are, Floyd, but just to simple people like you and I.
Physicists tend to look at things in a different manner."

"I believe it. Sorry I asked. Time for a break, five minutes
in every hour."

"You're on." I unstuck my canteen and took a swig, then
whistled to our dogtrotting terminal that was almost out of
sight. "Come back Fido, breakies."

"You're the boss," Aida said. The dog scrambled back,
barked and sniffed my pack where I had dropped it next to
me on the ground.

"Not too much realism!" I shouted. "Don't have that
plastic canine lift its leg on my pack!"

The day went on like that. Apparently forever. We crawled
across the landscape: the sun crawled across the sky. When we
had been walking for over five hours fatigue began to strike.
Floyd was striding ahead at a great pace.

"Tired yet?" I called out.

"No. Great fun."

"To those of us who weren't bashed about by the red
peril."

"Just a bit more."

The bit more went on a bit more than I appreciated and I was just about to toss in the towel when Fido spoke.

"Bow and wow, gentlemen. Just detected a couple of tachyons as they went whizzing by. Wasn't sure of the first one but—there it is, another—and another!"

"Coming from where?" I asked.

"Directly ahead. Let's just stay on this course and we'll track the source down. With, perhaps, yes I'm sure, there is the strong possibility of a course deviation later."

"Aha!" I aha'ed. "I recognize equivocation when I hear it. Even from a plastic dog mouthpiece for an ancient ship's computer."

"The word *ancient* is so hurtful . . ."

"I'll apologize when you tell me about this complication."

"Apology accepted. Allowing for the curvature of the planet, gravitic anomalies and other factors, I am still forced to believe that the tachyon source is not on the surface of this world."

"The thing is underground?"

"Underground is the very word for it."

I bit hard on the jawphone. "Tremearne, would you put the admiral on the line."

"*I'm here, Jim. Aida reported this possibility a while back and I have been monitoring developments since then. Didn't want to bother you, for all the obvious reasons.*"

"Yes, like we forgot to bring a shovel. Anything else you haven't told me?"

"*I was waiting for data, just coming in. I sent a low-flying probe to look for the gravimetric anomalies that Aida had found. Looks like there are a number of them and they are being plotted now.*"

"What kind of anomalies? Metal deposits?"

"*Quite the opposite. Caverns below the ground.*"

"It figures. Over and out. At least we now know where the artifact is."

"Where?" Floyd asked, since he had only heard my side of the conversation.

"Underground. There are caves or caverns of some kind up ahead. Nothing visible on the surface—but they are there all right. Our technical observers seem sure that the artifact is down there somewhere. Can we take that break now and wait for the reports?"

"I guess so."

Floyd guessed right, which was a good thing since an instant after we dropped to the ground the stream of bullets was fired at us. Zipping through the empty air where we had just been standing.

Floyd had a large and ugly pistol in his hand now which didn't slow him down as he wriggled on hands and knees beside me to the shelter of the mounded earth around a polpettone tree.

"We're under fire!" I shouted into my jawphone.

*"Source not visible."*

Fido stood on its hind legs—then jumped high into the air despite another burst of bullets.

"Bow-wow. Perhaps not visible to *others* but clear enough to me."

"What is it?"

"Some sort of apparatus at ground level. Want me to take it out?"

"If you can."

"Grrr!" it growled and retracted its legs, then zipped off at a great rate at ground level, so fast it could barely be seen. Moments later there was a muffled explosion and bits of debris rattled down into the shrub.

"That was quick," I said.

"Thank you," Fido said emerging from the undergrowth with a jagged bit of metal in its jaws. "Just follow me if you want to see the remains."

We followed the thing to a smoking pit with a jumble of

crumpled apparatus in its center. Fido dropped its bit of debris, lifted one front leg. Extended its head, straightened its
tail and pointed.

"Remote controlled gun turret. Note that the top of it is
camouflaged, concealed by dirt and sprouting plants. Hydrau-
lically operated—that's red oil not blood—to lift the apparatus
above ground level. Remains of an optical finder there. Note
the four automatic guns, Rapellit-binetti X-nineteens. Rate of
fire twelve hundred rounds a minute. Eighty rounds a second,
explosive and armor piercing."

"Since when have you been an armament authority,
Aida?" I asked.

"Since a long time back, sweetie-pie. In my heyday I was
required to know this sort of thing. I also know that these
particular guns have not been manufactured for over five hundred years."

# CHAPTER 23

I took another sip of water, wished that it was a stronger liquid. Was glad that it wasn't since a clear head was an important asset at this time.

"How old did you say these guns are?" I asked. There was no answer because our fake dog was digging away like a real dog throwing dirt behind it at a great rate. Burrowing down under the gun turret.

"Five hundred years old," Floyd said. "How can that be? Why use something that old?"

"You use it if that is all that you have. There is a mystery here that we are about to solve. Remember the ancient explosive that blew up the lab? It was also antique. So consider this. What if this planet had been settled before they started dumping societal debris on it? What if there were settlers here—only they were hidden away underground? It's a possibility. And if it is true, then it has been five centuries since they arrived. That's how long these mysterious migrants have been hiding away up here. Or down here, really. They must have been settled well before the League ever found this planet. That's why there is no record of them."

"Who are them?"

"Your guess is as good as mine . . ."

"Yarf!" our dogbot said, yarfing through a muzzle covered with dirt. "There is a fiber-optic cable going into the ground, obviously controlling this turret."

"Going down to the caverns. So, the next question—how do we get in . . ."

*"Jim,"* my jaw said. *"There is an interesting development taking place about three clicks away from you, in the same direction you have been walking. We've got image amplifiers on the electronic telescopes so we can see quite clearly . . ."*

"*What* can you see quite clearly?"

*"A group of armed men has emerged from some kind of opening in the ground. They appear to be dragging along one of their number who is bound. Now they are erecting a metal post of some kind. There is a struggle going on—apparently they are securing the bound man to the post."*

Memories of a thousand ancient flicks flooded my forebrain. "Stop them! It could be an execution—death by firing squad. Do something!"

*"Negative. We are in orbit. Short of launching an explosive torpedo, which is contraindicated at this time, there is nothing we can facilitate that will get there inside fifteen minutes at the very quickest."*

"Forget it!" I was digging into my pack as I whistled to the houndbot. "Fido! Catch!"

It jumped high and grabbed the gas bomb out of the air. "Go. Thataway. You heard the message—get to those guys and bite hard on that thing."

My last words were shouted in the direction of the tail that was vanishing among the shrubs. We grabbed up our packs and followed. Floyd easily outdistanced me and by the time I got to the scene, staggering and panting, it was all ancient history. Our faithful friend was barking and, foreleg lifted and tail outstretched, was pointing at the sprawled bodies.

"Well done, man's best friend," I said, and easily resisted the impulse to pat its plastic fur.

"For the record," I said for the benefit of my radio. "All males, all armed with shoulder weapons of some kind. There are twelve of them wearing camouflage uniforms. Thirteenth man—surely an unlucky number—tied to the post. No shirt."

*"Is he injured?"*

"Negative." I could feel a steady pulse in his neck. "We made it in time. Interesting, he's young, younger than the rest. What next?"

*"Decision made by the strategic planning computer. Take all weapons. Take the prisoner and remove him to a safe distance, then interrogate."*

I sniffed disdainfully as I unknotted the cords on the man's wrists. "Don't need a strategic planning computer to figure that one out."

Floyd caught him as he slumped free, threw him over his shoulder. I grabbed up the packs and pointed. "Let's get to that gully and out of sight."

The bomb that the ersatz hound had exploded was a quick in-and-out gas. One breath and you were asleep. For about twenty minutes. Which was all the time that we needed to hump our loads through the mud of the rain-eroded gully until we found a dry spot under an overhanging bank. Our prisoner —guest?—began to roll his head and mutter. Floyd and I, and our mascot, sat down to watch and wait. It wasn't long. He muttered something, opened his eyes and saw us. Sat half up and looked very frightened.

*"Fremzhduloj!"* he said. *"Amizhko mizh."*

"Sounds like really bad Esperanto," Floyd said.

"Just what you would expect if he and his kinfolk have been cut off from any outside contact for hundreds of years. Talk slow and he'll understand us."

I turned to him and raised my hands palms out in what I hoped was a universal sign of peace. "We're strangers, like you said. But what else did you say? Sounded like 'my friends'?"

"Friends, yes, friends!" he said, nodding like crazy, then shied away when Fido began barking.

"Aida, please. Will you shut your plastic poodle up. He's frightening our guest."

The thing stopped barking and spoke. "Just want to report that I am in contact with the watchers above. They report that the others who were rendered unconscious by the gas have regained consciousness and have retreated."

"Great. Just file everything and report later." I turned back to our guest—who looked very impressed by the talking-dog sequence. "Well, friend. My name is Jim and this is Floyd. The furry fake is Fido. You have a name."

"I am called Dreadnought, son of Impervious."

"A pleasure to meet you. Now—can you tell us why you were about to be wasted by that firing squad?"

"Disobeyment of orders. I was on Watch. Saw your group approaching. I fired the Watchturret at you—but do not yourselves anger! I aimed to miss. To fire demands permission of Watch Commander. That is why I was to be executed. I sought not his permission."

"Accidents happen."

"No accident. Fired because of orders."

"Are you following this?" Floyd asked.

"Not too well. Tell us, Dreadnought, who gave the order to fire if it wasn't the Watch Commander?"

"We all decided together."

"Who is *we*?"

"I can not tell you."

"Understandable. Loyalty to your friends." I clapped him on the back in a friendly manner and felt him shiver. "Getting cold. I'll get you a shirt."

I dug through my pack and took advantage of the opportunity for a muttered conversation with my jawphone.

"Any ideas? From you—or your indispensable strategic planning computer?"

*"Yes. If he won't talk to you perhaps the associates he re-*

*ferred to might be more communicative. Try to arrange a meeting."*

"Right." I went back with the shirt. "Here, Dreadnought, get out of the cold." He stood up and put it on. "Good. Now I've been thinking. I don't want you to tell me things that you are not supposed to. But maybe your friends, the ones you just told us about, maybe they can let us know what is going down. Can we meet them?"

He bit his lip and shook his head.

"No? Well let's try something else. Can you get back to your friends? Tell them about us. Talk about it. Find out if someone is prepared to tell us just what is happening. Okay?"

He looked from me to Floyd, even down at Fido who wagged its tail, before he made his mind up.

"Come with me."

He was young and strong and trotted along at a mean trot. Floyd and the mechanical mutt kept up fine but my aches and pains were coming back. I trailed behind and was going to call a halt when Dreadnought stopped at the edge of a grove of polpettone trees.

"Wait this place," he said when I had puffed and blown up to them. He twisted away among the trees. He didn't notice that Fido, legs folded, tail and head retracted, had slipped silently after him in the guise of a black floormop. The cessation of physical activity was welcome—as was the instant-heating meal I dug out of my pack. One porcuswine burger with gravy. Floyd popped his mealpak as well and we were licking the last drops of yummy from our fingers when the shadowlike mop reappeared. Legs, tail and head popped out and it barked. I scowled at it.

"Report first, bark later."

"Your new associate never saw me. Within the wood is a slab of rock that levers up with an opening beneath it. He went that way. Shall I show you where it is?"

"Later—if we have to. Right now let us take ten and see if he passes on our message."

Fatigue sat on me. I closed my eyes and took a lot more than ten. The sun was balancing on the horizon when I surfaced again. My computer obliged me by clicking the red six to a five when I checked the elapsed time. Don't worry, Jim— Admiral Steengo is on your side! This feeble reassurance didn't help and I was sure that I could feel the thirty-day poison beginning to bubble and seethe in my bloodstream.

Floyd was snoring lightly, sound asleep. Yet his eyes were open the instant Fido reappeared, disturbing some stones as it slid down the embankment.

"And a good-morning bow-wow to you gentlemen. Your new friend has emerged from under the lifting rock, along with an associate, and is coming this way. Remember—you heard it from me first."

Fido sat and waited, then barked a welcome when the two men appeared. They were nattily dressed in camouflaged uniforms and steel helmets, each helmet sporting a shiny spike on top. Bandoliers of bullets were draped over their shoulders, while there was a large and impressive handgun on each hip. But the guns were holstered and held in place by a buttoned strap. I relaxed knowing that with Floyd there the touch of a hand to one of those buttons would bring instant unconsciousness.

"Welcome back, Dreadnought," I said. "Welcome as well your companion."

"He is named Indefatigable and is the Area Commander. That is Floyd with the beard, the other is Jim."

Indefatigable did not shake hands but instead hit his closed right fist against his chest with an echoing thud. We did the same since it never hurts to learn the local customs.

"Why did you come here?" Indefatigable asked in a most cold and quizzical manner. I took slight umbrage.

"You might say we came to save your companion from certain death by the firing squad—your thanks are appreciated."

"If you had not come he would not have fired and have been condemned to death."

"Good point. But I do remember that he fired because of a group decision. Are *you* part of that group?"

I saw now that Indefatigable's brusque manner was a cover-up for the fact that he was very nervous. He chewed his lower lip and his eyes flicked from one to the other of us. He even looked down at the fake dog which barked. Finally, with great reluctance he spoke.

"I cannot answer that. But I have been instructed to take you to those who may answer your question. Now—you must answer my question. Why did you come here?"

"No point in keeping it a secret. We came here to find those who blew up a certain building and stole from it—and from us—an object of great importance."

This news seemed to relax him a bit. He stopped the lip chewing and Dreadnought almost smiled; leaned forward to whisper something in his companion's ear. They both nodded, then remembered where they were and snapped into a military brace.

"You will come with us," Indefatigable said, making it sound like an order.

"Perhaps," I said. I hate orders. "But you must tell us first —will it be dangerous?"

"We are born into danger; we leave it only when we die."

It sounded like a quotation of some kind—particularly since Dreadnought's lips moved along with his.

"Yes, well, that is a pretty general philosophical statement. But I was speaking specifically about like right now."

"You will be protected," he answered, trying to control the sneer at our feeble physiques and his obvious superiority.

"Oh, thank you," Floyd said with eye-popping sincerity. "With that kind of reassurance of course we will go with you. Isn't that right, Jim?"

"Absolutely, Floyd. With their protection we need not feel insecure." He could eat them—and a dozen more—for breakfast, but there was no point in bragging.

We reached for our packs but Indefatigable stopped us. "You bring nothing. No weapons. You must trust us."

Floyd shrugged agreement since he was always armed. "At least some water first," I said. Picking up my canteen and drinking a bit. Palming a number of small bombs as I put it back. "And of course our companion, our pet dog goes with us."

Fido played its role by barking, sticking out its tongue and panting. Then overplayed its role by lifting its hind leg on my pack. Though this bit of canine ham acting may have convinced our new militaristic mates, because they nodded agreement.

"We must cover your eyes," Dreadnought said, pulling out two black scarves. "So you do not discover the secret of the entrance to Shelter."

"If you mean the slab of rock under the polpettone trees that swings open, you can forget the blindfolds."

"How do you know this!"

"Just say that we do. Now—do we go with you?"

They looked stricken by my revelation, stepped aside and conversed in quick whispers. Returned reluctantly, all scowls again.

"You will come. Quickly."

We dogtrotted, including the dog, to the grove, then followed Dreadnought down the ladder into the tunnel beneath the slab. Fido barked, and when I looked up launched itself down at me. I caught it, then dropped it. Looked gloomily into the darkness as Indefatigable closed the lid.

I just hoped that we had made the right decision because my days were still running out. Going underground like this was a little too reminiscent of the grave.

And it would be my grave if I didn't get the antidote in time.

# CHAPTER 24

Once my eyes had adjusted to the darkness I saw that a thin line of light ran along at shoulder height on each side of the tunnel. The floor was smooth and hard, as were the walls when I brushed my fingers against them. We walked in silence for some time until we came to a cross tunnel.

"No talking now! Breathe silently—do not stir," one of our guides whispered. "Back against the wall."

We stayed that way for long minutes. I saw that there were glowing numerals on the walls where the tunnels crossed. I added to my store of useless knowledge the data that we were in tunnel Y-82790 at the place where it crossed NJ-28940. I leaned against the wall, and was thinking seriously about going to sleep, when I heard the thud of marching boots from NJ-28940. I woke up and remained silent and unmoving as a squad of about twenty men exited from the tunnel on our right and marched straight across and into the same numbered tunnel on the left. When the sound of their footsteps had almost died away we moved out to the whispered command.

"Turn left, after them. Quiet as you can."

This was apparently the only dangerous part of our journey, because once we had left this tunnel for another our companions whispered together again. I wondered if Fido was still with us.

"Don't bark," I said as softly as I could. "But if you are

still there, man's best friend, and hearing this with your super hearing, a tiny growl is permitted."

A guttural grrr sounded from somewhere around my ankles.

"Great. A double growl now if you are reading the tunnel numbers and memorizing same."

A quick grrr-grrr reassured me. So I did not have to keep track of our many turnings. After this we marched in silence for a tiresome period; my strength still wasn't what it should be. I was more than grateful when I saw a glow of light ahead; almost ran into our new companions when they stopped.

"Silence!" Dreadnought whispered. Floyd and I silenced and listened—then heard the running footsteps as well. They thudded close, then stopped suddenly.

"The sounds of deadly battle—" the newcomer said.

"Echo with the cries of the dying," Dreadnought answered. Password and countersign. Pretty depressing though. "Is that you, Irredeemable?" Dreadnought asked.

"It is. I was sent to warn you. A message was passed on from you-know-who that you were detected exiting and reentering the tunnels. Search parties are out and you must avoid them."

"How?" Indefatigable asked. With just a touch of hysteria to his voice.

"I do not know. I was sent only to warn. May the God of Battles go with you." With this blessing the footsteps thudded again into silence as he ran back the way he had come.

"What do we do?" Dreadnought asked unhappily. His companion was just as assertive. "I don't know . . ."

I swear that I could hear their teeth chattering. Whatever else they were, these two young men were not plotters or planners. Time for a pro to step in.

"I will tell you what we must do." Speaking as an unhumble old plotter and planner.

"What?" They spoke the word together.

"If they are searching the tunnels—then we must leave the tunnels."

"Wonderful," Floyd muttered. It may have seemed pretty obvious to him but these lads welcomed the idea as they would have orders from the God of Battles himself.

"Yes! Leave—before they find us!"

"Out of the tunnels!"

Good so far, I thought. When the silence lengthened, and I realized that was the end of their contribution, I asked the vital question.

"Out of the tunnels, right. But *where* do we go? Above ground again?"

"No—all exits will be watched."

"Only one other way," Dreadnought said, with rising enthusiasm. "Down, we must go down!"

"To the Cultivastings!" his companion added, just as filled with enthusiasm.

"Let's do it," I said wearily, not having the slightest idea of what they were talking about. "The God of Battles wants it that way."

They double-timed and we followed. Around the bend into the next tunnel where a glowing outline revealed that there was a metal door inset into the wall. Neither of our hosts tugged at the handle so there was a good chance that it was locked. Indefatigable stepped forward to face the illuminated keypad set into the wall beside it.

"Avert your eyes," he said. "The access code is top secret."

"Get it, Fido," I whispered. Aida reacted instantly; our plastic pet extruded sharp toenails, leaped high then climbed up my clothes, scratching my ear painfully as it jumped onto the top of my head. I resisted the temptation to say *ouch* and stood steady so it could read the punched-in numbers. The door creaked open and the creature jumped back to the ground.

A gentle breeze blew out through the doorway as we passed through it, smelling fresh and summery. Here underground? We stumbled in the darkness until the door clanged shut and the lights came on. We were in a small chamber facing a spiral staircase. Our hosts instantly started down it and we followed.

I was beginning to get dizzy from the round-and-round when we finally got to the bottom. The open door here glared with light. Blinking my tired eyes, I followed the others. Outdoors into a field of ripening corn. Startled birds flapped away when we emerged, while something small and furry disappeared among the stalks.

I knew that we couldn't possibly be outdoors, not after all the cave crawling that we had been doing. So this had to be a really giant cavern, with some kind of brilliant light sources above. These people really were independent of the surface— no wonder they hadn't been spotted before.

Dreadnought led the way between the rows of corn and we followed. It was hot and dusty, my fatigue was still there—and some species of tiny gnat kept trying to fly up my nose. I sneezed and rubbed and walked into Indefatigable's solid back when he stopped.

"Hail the Home and Joy in Survival!" he called out.

"Hail, hail and welcome, brave Defender," a voice answered.

A sweet and high-pitched woman's voice.

We started forward again and I stepped out from behind my guide's massive form, rubbing my nose and sniffling. I had a quick glimpse of a woman and three or four children working with hoes. It was a very quick glimpse—for the instant that she saw me she screamed.

"Invasion Day!"

It all happened incredibly fast. The children dived to the ground and she grabbed at the heavy pistol that hung from a lanyard around her neck. Raised it and began to fire at us.

We all hit the dust faster than the children had. Dread-nought was shouting, the gun was banging, rounds screamed by and exploded among the crops.

"Stop! No! No Invasion! Enough, enough!"

I don't think she heard him at all. I tried to crawl down through the topsoil while I saw her squeezing and squeezing on the trigger; her eyes round and terrified, white teeth sunk into her lower lip. The only thing that kept us alive was the fact that the gun kicked hard and the muzzle rode up into the sky, with the last shots vanishing into the zenith.

It ended just as quickly as it had started. The children had disappeared. Indefatigable had grabbed the gun away from her and was patting her on the back as she sobbed hysteri-cally.

"Well trained," Dreadnought said approvingly. "Irre-proachable is a fine woman, a good mother . . ."

"And thankfully a rotten shot," I said. "Would you like to tell us what all that was about?"

"Training. Survival. For lo these many generations. With the galaxy at war we seek only peace. We survive. They will kill themselves, but we will survive!"

He was winding himself up into a rallying speech so I broke in before he got into full spate.

"Stop! One minute—enough. The galaxy's wars and the Breakdown ended centuries ago. There is no more war."

He lowered his clenched fist and sighed; rubbed his knuckle across his nose. "I know. Some of us know. Most won't face the knowledge—cannot face it. We are too trained for survival and nothing else. Nothing in our programming and our lives has ever prepared us for a time without war. Without the threat of invasion. Some of us assemble, we talk, make decisions. About the future. We have a leader—I dare not tell you more!"

He broke off as Indefatigable came running back.

"The message has arrived—it is time to leave. The search has widened. If we move now we can stay behind the searchers and get to the meeting place. Quickly!"

We quicklied—and I was beginning to get very tired of it. The circular staircase had been a lot easier to come down than it was to climb up. Floyd saw my condition and if he hadn't half dragged me I doubt if I would have been able to make it. Once more into the black tunnels. I was only vaguely aware of our two guides, Floyd and the scuttling form of Fido. The next time we stopped I sagged against the wall. Enough was enough yet already.

"You will both stay here with Dreadnought," Indefatigable commanded. "You will be sent for."

Nor would our watcher answer any questions in the few minutes that we waited. "Proceed," a voice commanded and we did. Into a dimly lit chamber that appeared glaringly bright to our dark-adapted eyes. A half-dozen young men, garbed like our guides, sat on the other side of a long table.

"Stand here," Indefatigable ordered, then joined Dreadnought and sat down with the others.

"No chairs for us?" I asked, but was ignored. Fido felt equally irked, jumped up onto the table and barked. Jumped back to the floor to dodge the swing of a fist.

"Shut up," one of the men suggested. "We are awaiting orders. We are here, Alphamega."

They all turned to look at a red box on the table. It was made of plastic and was featureless except for louvers on one side.

"Are the two Outsiders you told me of present as well?" the box asked. The voice was flat and mechanical and obviously cycled through a speech occulter.

"They are."

"I speak to you, Outsiders. I have been told that you come here seeking an object taken from you."

"That is correct, speaking-box."

"What is the function of this object?"

"You tell me—you stole it from us." I was beginning to get teed off at all this cloak-and-dagger stuff.

"Your attitude is unacceptable. Answer my question or be punished."

I took a deep breath—and reined in my temper.

"I'd like that," Floyd said cheerfully, as fed up as I was with all this nonsense.

Where the discussion would have gone from here would never be known because at that moment running footsteps sounded and a wild-eyed young man burst into the room.

"Alarm! Watchpatrol coming!"

The sound of a number of thudding feet added a note of urgency to his warning. But at least our captors were prepared for the emergency. A door opened in the wall behind them and there was a rush to get through it. The newcomer, who must have known what would happen, was the last one in the crowd to jump to safety.

The table was in the way. I launched myself across it just in time to have the concealed door slammed in my face. I kicked it but it didn't budge. I looked at the now silent box.

"Speak up, Alphamega. How do we get out of this?"

The red box crackled—then burst into flame. Melted into a pool of plastic. "Thanks," I said.

"Any other way out?" Floyd asked.

"Not that I can see."

The rapid footsteps were just outside. Before I could dig out a gas bomb the scrum of armed men burst into the room.

Things got busy. Floyd dropped the first three who came through the door while I tackled the next two. Then the going got tough because more and more kept pushing in. Some had body armor, all of them had transparent riot masks attached to their spiked helmets. They didn't try to shoot us, but rather enjoyed clubbing us with their guns.

Something hard got me on the back of the head and I staggered and fell. Before they jumped me the last thing I saw was Fido going up the wall like a spider and vanishing in the darkness there. Then I got thudded and had a nice darkness of my own.

"Feeling any better, Jim?" a distant voice said and I felt something wet and cool on my forehead.

"Shbsha . . ." I said, or something like that. Chomped my dry mouth and opened my eyes. Floyd's face swam blurrily into view. I blinked and saw that he was smiling. He put the cold cloth back onto my forehead, which felt very nice.

"You got a bad one on the back of your head," he said. "They didn't hit me quite as hard."

I started to say *Where are we?* but figured that was a pretty dim question with an obvious answer. I could see a barred door which was hint enough. It hurt when I sat up on the bunk. Floyd handed me a plastic cup of water which I gurgled down and passed back for a refill. I patted my pockets and the seams of my trousers hopefully—but all my concealed weaponry was gone.

"Seen any dogs around lately?"

"Nope."

So that was that. Hit on the head. Imprisoned. Deserted by man's best friend. Somewhere underground so my jaw radio probably wouldn't work. Just in case I clacked hard and called for attention, but couldn't even get any static.

"Well—it could be worse," Floyd said in a repellently cheery fashion. I was about to curse him out when he got just the answer he deserved.

"And it will be. You will be dead," the man said from the other side of the barred door. "Instantly. If you attempt to touch me or the Killerbot behind me. Is that clear?"

He was gray-haired, stern-faced, dressed in the same combat fatigues and spiked helmet as everyone else whom we had

seen here. The only difference was that his spike was gold and
had stylized wings on it. He moved aside and pointed at the
very deadly-looking collection of mobile military hardware behind him. All guns, clubs, wheels, knives and metal teeth.
Teeth for tearing out throats?

I had no intention of finding out. "Follow me," our captor
said, turning and walking away. The cell door clicked and
swung open. Floyd and I shuffled out and followed him at a
discreet distance. Clanking and rattling, the Killerbot rumbled
along behind us.

The hallway, while being a depressing and drab tone of
gray, was at least well lit. At regular intervals were framed
photographs—apparently all of the same individual from what
I could see as we walked past. Or of a number of scowling
military types differing only in the braid and the medals on
their camouflage suits.

Our host turned into a doorway that was flanked by studded steel columns. We followed—all too aware of the clanking
apparatus just behind.

"Impressive," I said, looking around the giant chamber.
Black marble floor and walls. A large window looking out onto
a military camp filled with flapping flags, marching troops,
rows of armor-plated vehicles. Since we were deep underground it was obviously a projection—but a very good one.
These militaristic themes were also carried through in the inte-
rior decorations; light fixtures made of aerial bombs, machine-
gun flowerpots, draperies assembled from tattered, ancient
banners. I found it horribly depressing.

Without looking back our captor marched around the gigantic conference table and sat down in the single, high-
backed chair there. With a wave of his hand he indicated the
two smaller chairs before us.

"Sit," he commanded. Behind us was a clank and rattle, a
hiss of escaping steam. We sat.

Something brushed my ankle and I looked down and saw that padded clamps had swung into position to secure my legs; motors whirred and they tightened.

I threw my arms into the air just as clamps from the chair arms swung out and clicked shut on empty air.

"Not wise," our host said. There was a clank-clank close behind me and what could only have been a gun-muzzle ground into the back of my neck. The wrist clamps snapped open. I sighed and dropped my arms. I didn't have to look to know that Floyd had been imprisoned the same way.

"Leave."

When his master commanded the ambulatory war-machine clanked and rumbled out of the room and I heard the immense doors close.

"I am The Commander," our captor said, leaning back in his chair and lighting a large, green cigar.

"Is that your title or your name?" I asked.

"Both," he said, blowing a ring of blue smoke towards the ceiling. "I have imprisoned you since I do not wish to be attacked—nor do I wish to have anyone or anything present while we talk." He touched a button on his desk and looked at pulsing purple light. "And now we are secure against eavesdropping."

"Going to tell us who all you guys are, what you are doing here and that sort of thing?" I asked.

"Assuredly. We are The Survivalists."

"I think I heard a reference to your mob before."

"Undoubtedly. During the years of the Breakdown there were a number of groups with that name. We are the only ones who deserve it since we are the only ones who survive."

"Survivalists," Floyd said, and went on as though reading from a book. "Groups who believed in the inevitability of the coming war, as well as the inability of their own governments to protect them, who then withdrew from society into underground bunkers equipped with food, water, ammunition and supplies adequate to survive any catastrophe. None survive."

"Very good—you are quoting from . . . ?"

"Handbook of Historical Nuts, Cults and Saviors."

"Very good—except for the title and the last line. *We* survived."

"A little too well," I said. "The Breakdown Wars are long gone and the galaxy is at peace now."

"I'm glad to hear that. Just don't tell anyone else here."

"Why not? But let me guess. You want to keep them stupid and in line because you are onto a very good thing. For as long as there is war or the threat of war those in charge tend to stay in charge. Which, of course, is you."

"An excellent summation, Jim. Though there are those who are unhappy with the state of things . . ."

"We've met them. Youngsters who perhaps aren't too happy with the militaristic status quo and war forever. Who perhaps prefer a future in the bosom of their families. That is assuming you do have families?"

"Of course, safe and secure in the residential caverns. We guard them and protect them—"

"As well as having a generally good time playing soldier and bossing everybody about."

"Your criticism is becoming tiring."

He looked quizzically at his cigar ash, then tapped it into the ashtray before him. Which was made from a shell casing of course. Something black stirred at the very edge of my vision but I made no move to look that way. It was about time Fido made an appearance.

"So what do you want us for?" Floyd asked.

"I thought that was obvious. I want to find out who you are and how much you know about us."

There was a quick movement from under the table to my chair, out of The Commander's line of sight. The thing must have then climbed the back of my chair because Aida's voice whispered in my ear.

"I have done a voice analysis of a recording I made during the interrupted meeting. I stripped away the interference of the voice occulter and now know who the speaker who called himself Alphamega is . . . ."

"I already know," I said.

"Know what?" The Commander said. "What are you saying?"

"Sorry, just speaking my thoughts aloud. My thoughts being that you are playing some kind of complicated game, aren't you? You called me by name—and we have never been introduced. Of course if you were present at the meeting of the young dissidents you would know who I was. And now I know who you are."

I smiled and let the silence stretch before I spoke.

"The Commander—or Alphamega—which name do you prefer? Since you are both of them rolled into one."

# CHAPTER 25

"I can kill you—quite quickly," The Commander said coldly and calmly. But at the same time he was stubbing and crunching his cigar out in a most agitated manner.

"Temper, temper," I said. "Since you appear to be in charge of both sides in this internal conflict, and you obviously got us here for a reason—why don't you just tell us all about it?"

He was scowling now, angry and dangerous. As my mother always said—why was her memory still popping up?—you catch more porcuswine with honey than you do with vinegar. Gently, gently.

"Please, Commander," I pleaded most unctuously, "we're on your side, even when no one else is. You know exactly what you are doing—while none of your troops has the slightest idea what is happening. Not only are you in charge here, but it looks as though you have managed a mild insurrection on your own terms. You have done an incredible job that no one else was capable of doing. We can help you—if you will let us."

The scowl faded. Floyd followed my lead, smiled and nodded agreement and said nothing; another cigar was produced and lit. The smoke rose up and the smoker nodded beneficently.

"You are right of course, Jim. The responsibility has been great, the pressure continuous. And I am surrounded by morons—*stulteguloj, kretenoj!* Centuries of interbreeding and hiding underground has done little to improve their brain capacity. I am amazed that I alone have the intelligence to see this. I'm as different from them as if I had been born on a different planet, the child of superior parents."

This was sounding familiar. There has never been a strongman, dictator, military ruler, who did not believe that he somehow came from superior stock.

"You are different, sir," Floyd said, almost humbly. "I knew that as soon as you spoke."

We had both obviously read the same textbooks. Though I thought he was spreading it on rather thickly. I was wrong.

"You could see that? The difference is obvious I suppose, to someone from Outside. It hasn't been easy, I tell you. In the beginning I even tried to talk to the senior officers, explain some of the problems and suggest solutions. I could have had more communication talking to a wall. Not that the younger ones are any better. Though they are restless, give them that. When you get down to it there isn't much joy in just plain surviving. In the beginning maybe, it must have been a challenge then. But after a couple of centuries the pleasures begin to wear pretty thin."

"Was it the restlessness of the younger ones that gave you the idea to supply a leader for them to follow?" I asked.

"Not at first. But I began to see that the young were losing respect for the old. About the only people they looked up to were the scientists. From their point of view the scientists were the only ones who at least appeared to be doing new and important things. That's when I hit on the Alphamega role. They think that I am one of the younger scientists. A rebel who is unable to make any progress against the old ideas, the familiar ways—therefore I have been forced to enlist others of like age and mind."

"My arms are getting stiff," Floyd said, smiling. "You wouldn't mind taking off these clamps for a bit?"

"I would. I want you two just where you are."

Mercurial, our friend. All warmth gone in an instant, he dragged so hard on the cigar that it crackled and sparked. "We Survivalists watch events pretty closely—all over this planet. With a surveillance network set up before anyone else arrived. Amplified and spread ever since. Not a bird craps, not a polpettone fruit falls that we don't know about. That *I* don't know about. Because I watch the watchers. I watched and saw that a lot of energy and plenty of high-powered work was going into recovering that artifact. There is something very important about it—and I want to know just what. I had a squad steal it and destroy the building, hide their tracks. It was impossible to follow them. Yet you did. I want to know how you did that too. So talk—and talk fast."

"My pleasure," I said. "My friend here knows nothing about the artifact. But I do. I am the one who found it first, then tracked it and followed it here. I am the only one who can tell you how it operates—and what incredible things it can do. If you can take me to it I will be happy to show you how it works."

"That is more like it. You will come with me. Your associate remains here as a guarantee—don't you agree?" He stood and buckled on a large and offensive-looking sidearm.

"Of course. Sorry about that, Floyd," I said as I turned my head to face him. Winking with my left eye, the one our captor couldn't see. "I know that you would come after me and help me if you could. But you can't. So stay here and you will be safe. You have the word of James Fido diGriz on that."

"I'll be okay, Jim. Look after yourself."

I only hoped that this mixture of innuendo, hints and suggestions had delivered my message to him. I could only cross mental fingers and hope. The door opened and there was a hiss, rumble and clank behind me as my bonds snapped open. I rubbed my stiff arms and stood up slowly and carefully. The Killerbot blinked baleful little orange eyes at me and waved a smoke-stained flamethrower in the direction of the door. I followed Commander Alphamega out, leaving Floyd prisoner in the chair. Not for long, I hoped, if Fido-Aida had understood my suggestions.

We walked side by side down the wide hall with its framed portraits of heroes. My companion smiled warmly in my direction. Pulling his gun a bit out of the holster at the same time, then letting it slide back.

"You do understand that if you breathe one word about our conversation you will be no more than a grease spot on the floor?"

"Completely aware, thank you. Absolute silence on that topic, yes, sir. I will look at the artifact and explain its operation. Nothing more."

Maybe I was smiling on the outside—but I was pretty gloomy on the inside. Jim, you are getting yourself in deeper than a porcuswine in a mudhole. A depressing thought—and a true one. But I really had no choice.

It was quite a long walk and I was getting tired again. When all this was over—*if* it were ever over—I promised myself a nice long holiday. Head-up, Jim! Think positive and get ready to improvise.

A last door opened and we were in what was obviously a laboratory. Complete with control boards, power cables, bubbling retorts and aged scientists in white smocks. There was a lot of loyal fist-smacking on chests when the leader appeared. Salutes that he returned with the merest tap of his own loosely clenched fist. They moved respectfully back to give us access to a lab bench. On it, now sprouting wires and connections to the surrounding test gear, was the alien artifact. I clapped my brow and staggered.

"What are you cretins doing with the cagleator!" I shouted. "We are all dead if you have actuated it!"

"No, no—not that!" an elderly scientist cackled. Then shut up and looked fearfully at the Commander who sneered in return.

"You are all morons. Now tell this Outsider what you have done," he ordered. "He is the one who knows what the device can do."

"Thank you, thank you! Of course, as you have ordered." The wrinkly turned back to me with shaking hands and pointed a quavering finger. "We have only X-rayed the device and charted the circuitry. Very complex, as you know. There was, however . . ." he began to sweat, looking about unhappily, "a reaction of some kind when we attempted to test the circuitry."

"A reaction? If you have made a mistake the world has just ended! Show me."

"No, not a big reaction. Just that it absorbed electricity from our test circuit. We were not aware of this at first—and we instantly terminated the test when we saw what was happening."

"And just *what* did you see happening?" The Commander asked, voice like a file on rough steel.

"That, sir, we saw that. A cover of some kind fell away disclosing this recess. And the lights. That is all. Just lights . . ."

Fascinated, we all leaned forward to look. Yes, there was the recess. And inside it there were four little blobs of light. Green, red, orange and white.

"What is the significance of this?" my inquisitor asked, fingers strumming on the gunbutt.

"Nothing important," I said, stifling a yawn at the unimportance of it all. "The test circuitry is simply testing the circuits of your test circuitry."

I poked out a casual finger towards the glowing lights and found the barrel of his weapon grinding into my side.

"That sounds like absolute waffle to me. The truth, *now,* or you are dead."

There are seconds that sometimes appear to stretch for a length of time bordering on eternity. This was one of those occasions. The Commander glared at me. I tried to look innocent. The scientists, slack-jawed, looked at him. The Killerbot waited in the doorway and clanked to itself, hissing steam and probably wishing that it was killing something. Time stood still and eternity hovered close by.

I had very few options open.

Like none.

"The truth is . . ." I said. And could not go on. What could I possibly say that would impress this maniac in any way? At this moment there was a great explosion and pieces of Killerbot clanked and rattled in through the door.

As you might imagine this really did draw everyone's attention. As did the voice that rang out an instant later.

"Jim—drop!"

And there was Floyd at the open door, brandishing an impressive weapon of some kind. Fido has done its job and freed him. He had polished off the Killerbot and was now taking the action from there.

The Commander swung his weapon around, raised it, ready to fire.

I did not drop as instructed because I was possessed by a hallucinatory moment of madness. I had been pushed around too much of late and suddenly, overwhelmingly, felt like doing a little pushing back.

The lights in the artifact glowed their welcome and my finger punched out in their direction.

To do what?

To touch one of the beckoning colored lights, of course.

Which one?

What color meant what to the ancient aliens who had built this thing?

I had no idea.

But green had always meant *go* to me.

Cackling hysterically I stabbed down on the green light . . .

# CHAPTER 26

Apparently nothing happened. I pulled my finger back and looked at the lights. Then at The Commander and his drawn gun, wondering why he hadn't used it.

Then looked at him again. And saw that he wasn't moving. I mean just not moving in the slightest. I mean like paralyzed. Petrified. Glassy-eyed and frozen.

As was everyone else in the room. Floyd stood in the doorway, gun raised and mouth open in an endless shout. Behind him, for the first time, I noticed an unmoving Fido.

The world was a freeze-frame and I was the only one not trapped in it. I was surrounded by people stopped in the act of speaking, walking, moving. Off-balance, hands raised, mouths gaping. Now stilled, silent—dead?

I started towards The Commander, to relieve him of his gun—saw that his finger was tight on the trigger! But with each step I felt the air resisting my movement, growing firm, then more solid until it was like walking into an unyielding wall. Nor could I breathe—the air was a thick liquid that I could not force into my lungs.

Panic grew and grabbed me—then died away just as quickly when I stepped back. I felt normal again. Air was air and I breathed in and out quite nicely.

"Put the mind in gear, Jim!" I shouted at myself, my words loud in the surrounding silence. "Something is happening—but what? Something happened after you touched the green light. Something to do with the artifact."

I stared at it. Tapped it with my knuckles. Groped about for inspiration. Found it.

"Tachyons! This thing emits them—we know that because that is how Aida tracked it in the first place. Tachyons—the units of time . . ."

The device was now functioning—I had turned it on when I had pressed the light. Green for go. Go where?

Stasis or speed. Either I had been speeded up or the world had slowed down. Or how could I tell the difference? From my point of view everything seemed to have slowed and stopped. The artifact had done something, projected a temporal field or stopped the motion of molecules. Or had created an occurrence that froze the surrounding world in a single moment of time. Time had come to a stop everywhere that I could see—except in the close vicinity of the device. I moved even closer and patted it.

"Good little time machine. Time mover, slower, halter, stopper—whatever you are. Neat trick. But what do I do next?"

It chose not to answer me. Nor did I expect it to. This was my problem now and I had to force myself to take the time to think it out. For the moment I had all the time I needed. Though eventually I would have to do something. And that something would probably mean touching another one of the colored buttons. Either that or I could stand looking dumbly at the device while I quietly died of thirst or starvation or whatever.

But which light?

Green had been obvious enough—even more obvious by hindsight. And the decision had been made at a moment of life and death. Now I was not so sure. I reached out, then dropped my hand. With plenty of time to decide I had become the master of indecision. Green had meant go, turn on, get started. Did red mean off, stop? Maybe. But what about white and orange?

"Not an easy one, Jimmy boy?" I said in what I hoped was a jocular voice—which came out very mournful and doom-laden. I wrung my hands together with indecision. Then stopped and looked at them as though I might see some answer printed on my fingers. All I saw was dirt under the nails.

"You have got to do it sooner or later—so do it sooner before your nerve fails completely," I told myself. Reached out a finger—drew it away. It looked like my nerve had indeed failed me completely.

"Take yourself in hand, Jim!" I ordered. Reached back and took a handful of collar and shook myself as violently as I could.

It was no help at all. Random choice then? Why not, just as good as guessing. I put the finger out again and promised myself that I would push down on whatever color was under the finger when the jingle ended.

"Eeeny, meeny, miney, shmoe, catch a . . ."

I never found out what I was going to catch because at that moment I heard the dragging footsteps coming from the hall.

Sound?

Out there where nothing moved!

I jumped about, hands raised in defense. Lowered them and waited as the footsteps grew louder, came closer and closer to the doorway . . .

Slipped past Floyd's immobile body.

"Aliens! Monsters!" I gasped, pulling back. Trying to run although I knew there was no place to go.

Two hideous metal creatures. Bifurcated limbs, many-angled skulls, glowing eyes, claw-fingered hands. Coming towards me. Stopping. Reaching out—

No! Reaching up to twist their own heads off. I could hear a gurgling scream, was only dimly aware that it was my own voice.

Twisted and turned and lifted—

Lifted off the helmets. Two very human faces looked at me with a good deal of interest. I stared back with the same emotion. Realized that, despite the close-cropped hair, the one on the left was female. She smiled at me and spoke.

*"Wes hal, eltheodige, ac hwa bith thes thin freond?"*

I blinked, didn't understand a word. Shrugged and smiled in what I hoped was a winning way. The second visitor shook his head.

*"Unrihte tide, unrihte elde, to earlich eart thu icome!"*

"Look," I said, having enough of this and very much needing a few questions answered. "Could you please try Esperanto? That good, old, simple intergalactic second language Esperanto."

"Certainly," the girl said, smiling a winning and white-toothed smile. "My name is Vesta Timetinker. My companion is Othred Timetinker."

"Married?" I asked for some incomprehensible reason.

"No, stepsiblings. And you—you have a name?"

"Yes, of course. James diGriz. But everyone calls me Jim."

"A pleasure to meet you, Jim. Our thanks for activating the temporooter. We'll take it off your hands now."

She started towards the artifact—which I now knew was a temporooter. Though I still knew little else. I stepped in front of it and said:

"No."

"No?" Her rather attractive forehead furrowed while Othred's face suddenly looked grim. I turned a bit so I could keep an active eye on him.

"If *no* is too abrupt," I said, "then I will ameliorate it and say hold on just a moment if you please. Didn't you just thank me for finding this thing?"

"I did."

"Finding means that it has been lost. And has now been

recovered because of my intervention. In return for this favor I believe you owe me at least an explanation."

"We're dreadfully sorry. But it is strictly forbidden to pass on information to temporal aborigines."

Not too flattering, I thought. But I was thick-skinned enough to take it. "Look," I carefully explained. "This is one aborigine who already knows a good deal about what is happening. I now have in my possession your temporooter, a device that has been constructed for burrowing through time. It seems that you or your associates not only lost control of the device but actually lost it in time and space. This is very worrying because you are forbidden to reveal your operations to people living along the time tracks you explore."

"How—how do you know this?" she asked. Well done, Jim. They may be long on linguistics but are certainly short on extrapolation and imagination. Keep going.

"At first, when we aborigines discovered the device, we thought it was an alien construction from the far past, built by long-lost, millennia-dead aliens. Of course the real explanation is much simpler. It was sent from the *future* and through a malfunction got out of control." Now I was just guessing—but their shocked expressions meant I was still doing well.

"Got so far out of control that it just kept going back in time until it ran out of power. Without power you could not locate it. You thought it might have been destroyed. Which is why there was such consternation when it signaled its presence. And you two were sent to retrieve it."

"You—you read minds?" She spoke in a hushed voice. I nodded firmly.

"The science of mental telepathy is well advanced in this era. Though it is obvious that all knowledge of our abilities has been expunged from your records in the future. But I will cease my mind reading now. I know how embarrassing it is to have one's secret thoughts revealed to strangers." I turned away, pinched my forehead, turned back. "I have stopped the function. We now communicate by words."

They looked at each other, still dazed.

"Speak, please, for now I do not know what you are thinking. Only by speech can we understand each other's thoughts."

"Knowledge of time travel is forbidden," Othred said.

"That's not my fault—you're the ones who lost the thing. You must understand that now I know all about it—as do all of my brothers in telepathekinesis who have been listening to my thoughts. But we are sworn to silence! If you wish your secret to remain a secret it will be secret. But you must aid us in keeping this secret secret. Look about you. See this ugly-looking type in the horned helmet? He is just about to kill me. And when you entered you probably stepped over the wreckage of a very armed and deadly machine—you did?, nod yes—good. That thing was going to kill me and my friend, but he got it first. So just turning off the temporooter and skedaddling is out of the question. You will leave behind a deadly and destructive situation."

"What must we do?" Vesta asked. Palm of my hand.

"First you will help me by permitting myself and my associates to escape before the time stasis has been turned off."

"That should be possible," Othred said.

"Then that's agreed. Secondly I will need another temporooter to take back with me . . ."

"Forbidden! Impossible!"

"Hear me out, will you please. Another temporooter to take back that *does not function*. A realistic fake that will disguise the fact that you and your machine have been here. Catch on?"

"No."

They sure bred them dumb in the future. Or without imagination or whatever. I took a deep breath.

"Look. I want you to remember that all the scientists here, in this time, know that there is a device of some kind that looks like your temporooter. Only they think that it is an alien artifact from the far past. Let us convince them that their assumption is true. If we do that, why no one will ever know about you and your lost equipment. Just have your technicians get some million-year-old rock and carve out something that looks like this. We'll pass it off as the original, the secret will be kept, honor satisfied, all's well that ends well."

"Excellent idea," Vesta said, and pulled a microphone from her armored suit. "I'll have one constructed now. It will be here in a second or two—"

"Wait. I have another small favor to ask. I will need certain functions built into the duplicate to convince our scientists that it is not a dummy. Just a simple device that will destruct after a single operation. This will pose absolutely no difficulties for your techs, I am sure."

It took me a bit longer to convince them of this necessity, but in the end they reluctantly agreed. The duplicate was an exact physical duplicate of the original. It blinked into existence floating in the air before us. Othred reached up and tugged; there was a popping sound as he pulled it down and handed it to me.

"Wonderful," I said, tucking it under my arm. "Shall we go?" They nodded agreement and put their helmets back on.

I had my temporal companions first release the stasis field on Floyd's hand so I could disarm him. Like our mutual enemy his finger was also tightening on the trigger. What a world of nascent danger we do live in! I tucked the gun into my belt and nodded to the tempotechs.

Give Floyd that—his reflexes were great. He was twisting and chopping towards Othred's neck the second he moved— stopped when I called a halt.

"Friends, Floyd. Down boy! Ugly-looking monster friends

who are getting us out of here. If you look around you, you will see that all our enemies are paralyzed with indecision—and will stay that way until we are gone. Don't trip over the pieces of the Killerbot on the way out. And, Vesta, if you please. Tap that fake ball of fur with your magic wand so it can join us."

"What the hell is going on?" Floyd said, blinking in confusion as he tried to understand what was happening.

"I feel that some explanation is in order," Aida said, and Fido barked with exasperation.

"Second the motion," Floyd said.

"Forthcoming. As soon as we are out of here. Will you be so kind as to lead the way back to the surface."

I turned to thank my temporal saviors, but they were already gone. Not only short on imagination but bereft of manners as well. And when they had vanished they had taken the time stasis with them; I could hear our footsteps for the first time. I looked back with a sudden feeling of horror but, right, the stasis was still working for the enemy as the silent form of the gun-toting snarling Commander indicated.

"Time to leave," I said. "Since I have no idea how long the nasties are going to stand around that way. Go!"

"Explain!" Floyd shouted. Not in the best of moods.

"In a moment," I equivocated—and stopped dead. For I had suddenly been possessed of an even more horrifying idea. All this playing with time—what had it done for my personal poisonous deadline! I groped for my pendant skull-computer but of course it was gone with the rest of my equipment. How much time had passed? Was the poison now taking effect? Was I about to die . . . ?

Sweating and trembling I dropped the replacement artifact temporooter and grabbed up the plastic poodle.

"Aida—is Fido transmitting?"

"Of course."

"What time is it—I mean what day? No cancel that command. Get on to the Admiral now. Ask him how much time I have left. When is the deadline? Now—please. Don't ask me any questions. He'll know what you are talking about. Do it! And fast!"

Time dragged by on very sluggish feet I will tell you. Floyd must have heard the desperation in my voice for he stayed silent. A second, a minute—a subjective century crawled by before I had my answer. Aida must have done it—and made a good connection. Because the next voice Fido spoke with was that of Admiral Steengo.

"Good to hear from you, Jim . . ."

"Don't talk. Listen. I don't know what day it is. How much time is there to the deadline?"

"Well, Jim, I wouldn't worry about that if I were you—"

"You are *not* me and I am worried and answer the question or I will kill you slowly first chance I have. Speaking of killing . . ." I found that I couldn't go on.

"I meant it when I said don't worry. The threat of the thirty-day poison is over."

"You have the antidote?"

"No. But the thirty days are past. Two days ago!"

"*Past!!* Then I'm dead!"

But I wasn't dead. My brain spluttered and clanked and slipped back into gear. Thirty days past. No antidote. I was alive. I could hear my teeth grating as I spoke.

"Then the thirty-day poison—the whole thing was a fake from the start, wasn't it?"

"I am afraid that it was, and I do apologize. But you must realize that I did not know about it until now. Only one person had that information, the instigator of the operation."

"Admiral Benbow!"

"I'm afraid that information is not mine to reveal."

"You don't have to—it reveals itself. That lawyer who gave

me the drink was just doing as directed. Lawyers will do anything if you pay them enough. Benbow was in charge and Benbow invented the poison plot to keep me in line."

"Perhaps, Jim, perhaps." His voice, even when transmitted through the agency of a plastic dog, reeked of insincerity and equivocation. "But there is nothing we can do about it now. A thing of the past. Best forgotten. Correct?"

I nodded and thought—then smiled. "Correct, Admiral. Why don't we just forget about the whole thing. All's well that ends well and tomorrow is another day. Forget it."

*For now,* I thought to myself, but did not speak that important little codicil aloud.

"I'm glad you understand, Jim. No hard feelings then."

I dropped the dog, turned and clapped Floyd happily on the shoulder, bent and picked up the replacement artifact.

"We did it, Floyd, we did it. I will explain everything as we walk. In great detail. But as you can see we are free, in possession of this artifact. Mission accomplished. Now—lead on, faithful Fido, since you have memorized the entrance-and-exit path. But go slowly, for it really has been one of those days."

I was hungry and thirsty. But even more thirsty for—what? Revenge? No, revenge was a dead end. If not vengeance—what then?

The time had come for a little evening up, a little sorting out of the record. I had been taken in completely by the poisonous con job. So before the last *i* was dotted, before the last alien artifact laid to rest, I was going to see that a little justice got done.

On *my* terms.

# CHAPTER 27

"Carry this for a bit, will you Floyd," I said, passing over the replacement temporooter. We were leaving the last lit tunnel behind and would depend now on Aida to remember the way. "I'm a little on the tired side."

"I don't wonder. But you have to understand—my patience has just run out. So work hard and see if you can dig up enough energy to tell me just what happened. I am now completely confused. I remember that I wasted the Killerbot with that gun you now have tucked into your belt, the one Fido brought to me. Then I jumped through the door and told you to get down so I could blast the Commander as well as anyone else who was looking for trouble."

"That's just the way I remember it."

Fido barked and turned a corner from one dark tunnel into another even darker one. Floyd sounded worried.

"I remember pulling the trigger—then suddenly you are holding the gun, not me, and right next to me there are two creatures, people, robots, something like that. I blink and look into the lab and everyone is standing like they are frozen. Nothing moves—but nothing. Then when I look back I see that the two metal things have vanished. So I am beginning to feel like I am going around the mental bend. Therefore I would appreciate it if you would kindly, and quickly, tell me what happened."

"I wish I knew. I saw the same things you did. I don't know what happened."

"But you *must* know—you were talking to them!"

"Was I? I don't remember. Everything is still kind of fuzzy."

"Jim—don't do this to me. You *have* to remember! And what were you shouting at the Admiral about? Something about poison and another Admiral."

"That's easy enough to answer. Certain individuals blackmailed me into this operation by telling me I had been poisoned and that I had thirty days to live if I didn't get the antidote. There was no poison—therefore no antidote. So all the time we have been rushing about I have been thinking about the poison and counting the days before I curled up my toes and keeled over."

He was silent a moment, then he spoke.

"That's pretty heavy. You are sure about that?"

"I am. And I am also terminally tired so can we please put this conversation off for a bit. I would just like to concentrate on putting one foot in front of another for awhile."

Like it or not Floyd had to settle for that for the moment. Because I needed some time for deep cogitation, to dream up some sort of reasonable story for him—as well as the rest of the troops. Stumbling with fatigue I was grateful that we made our way through the tunnels without meeting any opposition. Though I had the gun ready just in case. When Fido actuated the escape hatch and it opened to reveal the blue sky—I sighed with relief. Gave the gun back to Floyd and used my remaining strength to crawl out onto the ground. Dropped with a groan and leaned back against a polpettone tree.

"You have the gun, Floyd," I said. "So pass me back that ancient artifact if you please. Aida—is there any transportation on the way?"

"There should be. I sent out your position as soon as you were aboveground and I could get a triangulation. Help is on the way."

As indeed it was—for a black spot in the sky grew quickly into the launch from the good old *Remorseless*. It landed with a shuddering thud, which bit of flying I recognized, so I was not surprised when Captain Tremearne exited through the open door.

"Congratulations," he said, and stuck out his hand. "You did it, Jim."

"Thanks," I said, as he gave my hand a good crushing handshake. "And don't think that it was easy."

"Never! I was there—remember. Can I relieve you of that thing?"

"No!" I shouted—and was shocked to hear the fine edge of hysteria, or incipient madness, to my voice. Well why not! "I'll hand it over—along with a detailed explanation of just what it is—at the meeting."

"What meeting?"

"The meeting that you are now going to arrange at the Pentagon. I'll want all The Stainless Steel Rats there. A last reunion so to speak. Has Madonette gone back to her imprisoning office yet?"

"She was supposed to. But she would not leave the planet until you came back."

"Faithful to the end! So in addition to all the Rats I would like a few other friends present."

"Friends?" He looked baffled. "Like who?"

"Well that macho fat thug Svinjar for one. King of the Machmen. Then you can invite Iron John and his opposite number, Mata. Ask yourself to come along as well. It will make an interesting gathering."

"Interesting—yes! But impossible. None of the exiles on this prison planet is permitted inside the Pentagon."

"Really? I thought that you were the guy that was going to see that Liokukae was cleaned up and cleaned out?"

"Yes—but—"

"Now is the time, Captain. For at this meeting I am not

only going to turn over the alien artifact and reveal its secret—but I am going to tell everyone just how the situation here is going to end."

"How?"

"You're invited to the meeting. You'll hear then."

"This will not be easy to arrange."

"Yes it will." I pointed to Floyd. "Ask him about the strange things that happened when we were back there with the Survivalists. Admiral Steengo will verify his reports. There is a lot more to be cleaned up on this planet than you ever realized. Get your arguments together, consult your superiors, look after this." I passed over the artifacted artifact. "And don't wake me up until it has been all arranged."

I climbed wearily into the launch. Pushed up the armrests on the back row of seats. Stretched out and fell instantly to sleep.

The next thing I knew Floyd was shaking me gently by the arm. "We're back in the Pentagon. The meeting is on just like you said. I have breakfast and some clean clothes waiting for you. They'll be ready when you are."

The shower blasted out warm water and heated air and I stayed under it far too long. But it did wonders not only for my disposition but for my sore muscles as well. I did not hurry. They had arranged the meeting—on my terms—only because they had no choice. They would have informed me to get stuffed if they could. But the labtechs would have found nothing when they examined the artifact. Floyd would have told his confused story about what had happened when he had jumped in with his gun ready. Very confusing. In the end they would have been forced to the reluctant conclusion that the only way they could ever find out what had happened in the underground laboratory was by having me tell them. After which, knowing their record for veracity, they probably felt that they could do whatever they wanted with me.

"Well, Jim," I said to my smiling and sleek image in the mirror, as I carefully combed my hair, "let's give them what they want."

Floyd was my guide. Stamping in step with me along the corridors and into the conference room.

"Hi, guys!" I said in cheery greeting to the far-from-friendly faces.

Only Madonette returned my smile, waved a tentative hand. Admiral Steengo was stern, Tremearne uncommunicative—as was Mata. Floyd was grim-faced—but winked when I glanced his way. Iron John and Svinjar were chained to their chairs or they would have killed me instantly. As it was they strained forward, eyes bulging with homicidal rage. I was most pleased to see that my hairy red friend had a bandaged skull and an arm in a sling. The aged artifact lay on the table before them and I went and sat on the edge of the table next to it.

"Tell us about the device," Admiral Steengo said in a reasonable and friendly voice.

"Not quite yet, Admiral. I assume that your techs could make nothing of it?"

"They say it is over a million years old. That's all."

"There's more to it than that. But first a few introductions. The bruised guy with red fur is Iron John. Leader of a cult which you are now going to abolish. You can ship him off for treatment at an establishment for the criminally insane. Along with the fat man next to him. I have them here because I wanted you to see just what your policies of benign neglect had forced on the human beings out there on garbage world."

I smiled and waited for the cursing and the spitting to die down, then nodded pleasantly at the unwholesome twosome.

"Would anyone here like to live in the kind of societies that you are subjecting the helpless people on Liokukae to? A committee must be appointed now. Plans drawn up to free the women and children from their bondage. You will find that Mata will be able to advise you on that. I think the various males on the planet will have to be interviewed separately. I'm sure that a number of them like their world the way it is. They can have it. The others deserve something better. But all that is in the future. First let us look at the past. I'm sure that the others on my team will grieve the passing of The Stainless Steel Rats. We have played our last gig, sung our last song. And we did pretty well for a bunch of amateurs. One juvenile criminal. An admiral, an unarmed combat expert, and a—what are you really, Madonette? And don't embarrass both of us by talking about the imaginary office job again. That's not your style. Everyone else has come clean—so how about you?"

She drew herself up, looked grim—then smiled. "You deserve the truth, Jim. My office really is out there. But it is in the Galaksia Universitato where I teach in the department of archeology. The university has so much money involved in this operation that they insisted on a representative."

"I'm glad it was you, Professor. Been fun working with you." I blew her a kiss, which she snatched out of the air and blew back.

"I didn't know about this!" Admiral Steengo said, more than miffed. "I am beginning to find out that there are levels of secrecy and duplicity in this so-called artifact retrieval operation that no one seems to know anything about. The more I discover about it—the more it stinks. And more and more it appears to bear the stamp of Stinky Benbow."

"That nickname is classified and will be stricken from the records," a loathsomely familiar voice grated from the direction of the suddenly opened door. "Fun and games are over. Sit down diGriz. I am in charge now."

"Well as I live and breathe!" I turned, filled with great pleasure, to face the ever-scowling countenance of Admiral Benbow. "This is almost too good to be true. The old poisoner himself—in person."

"You will be silent. That is an order."

Steengo was shocked. "Benbow, you bastard—have you

been going over my head with this project? Are there other things about it that even I don't know?"

"Plenty. But your need to know is plenty far down the knowing chain of command. So, like this crook—shut up."

"No more orders, Benbow," I broke in. Reluctantly since there is nothing I enjoy more than a brace of admirals slanging each other off. But this was a time for work, not fun. "Now tell the truth, just for a change. It was your idea to give me the fake thirty-day poison, wasn't it?"

"Of course. I know how to deal with criminals. No trust, just fear. And complete control." The lizard lips bent into a frigid smile. "I will show you how it works."

He snapped his fingers and an aide hurried in with a familiar package. He held it up and the serpentine smile broadened. "You didn't really think that I would let you get away with this, did you?"

It was the package with the three million credits that I had mailed to Professor Van Diver for safekeeping. My fee for putting my life in danger, money well earned. Now in the hands of the enemy. Not only wasn't I bothered by seeing it—I was overjoyed.

"How kind of you, dear Admiral," I chortled. "The circle is complete, the ring closed. The play ended. The alien artifact retrieved. The last song sung. Thank you, thank you."

"Don't sound so cheery, diGriz—because you are in the deep cagal. Although you will not be executed for robbing the Mint you *will* get a well-deserved prison sentence for that crime. This fee, which you extorted from the university, will be returned to them. Along with that artifact . . ."

"Oh—so we have remembered it at last. Don't you want to know what it is, what it does?"

"No. Not my problem. Let the university worry about that. I was against this entire operation from the first. Now it is over and life will go on the way it was."

"Including life on this despicable planet?"

"Of course. We are not going to let the do-gooders interfere with the sound administration of the law."

"Admiral—I do admire you," I said, standing and turning
to the intent audience. "Hear that, Iron John? You can go
back to your old job at the bottom of the pond as soon as your
bones heal. Svinjar, more killing and general swinery on your
part. There will be the return of the rule of law and justice—
on Admiral Benbow's terms."

"Arrest this man," Benbow ordered, and two armed
guards entered and marched towards me.

"I'll go quietly," I said. Turned and touched the alien artifact as I had been instructed to. "But I'll go alone."

It was so quiet you could heard a pin drop. But, of course,
a pin could not drop.

Nothing could move, was moving. Would move for quite a
while.

Except me, of course. Strolling over, cheerfully whistling
"Nothing's Too Bad for the Enemy," relieving the Admiral of
my hard-earned fee. Smiling benignly into his glaring, frozen
face. Due to stay that way for quite awhile. I turned and waved
at my statue-like audience.

"The best part was working with The Stainless Steel Rats.
Thanks guys. Thanks as well to you, Captain Tremearne. In
fact—not only thank you—but could you give me a little
help?"

I walked over and touched his arm as I said this, enclosing
him in the stasis-resistant field that enveloped me.

"Help you do what?" He looked around at the motionless
scene, turned back to me. "What's going on here?"

"What you see is what you get. No one is hurt, but no one
is going to move for some time. Temporal stasis. When they
come out of it they will never know that they have been in it."

"This is what happened to Floyd?"

"Exactly."

"Exactly what?"

"Time travelers. The alien artifact is not alien at all—but a human construct from the far future, sent back and lost in time. I promised the time travelers not to tell anybody. I'll make this single exception since I need your help."

"Doing what?"

"Getting both of us out of here so we can start the job of cleaning up this putrid planet. Here is what we have to do. Admiral Benbow has just arrived, as you saw, which means there is an interstellar spacer up there now in orbit about this planet. You and I will grab some transportation and get up to it. Once there you will use your rank, guile and forceful manner to see that we get aboard and far away from Liokukae. Then, when we get back to civilization, we will generate plenty of publicity about the evils men do here on this planet. It will be a scandal and heads will roll."

"Mine will be the first. Along with a court-martial, possible flaying and certainly life imprisonment."

"It shouldn't be that bad. If we get the forces of light on our side, why then the forces of darkness won't be able to lay a finger on you."

"It will take time . . ."

"Captain—that's the one thing we got plenty of! A good six months of it. That's how long this stasis will last. They won't know it, will not even realize a single second has passed. But, oh, will there be consternation among them when they discover how things have changed while they have been dozing! When I leave here the stasis will seal itself, impenetrable and impermeable. By the time it lifts the reform campaign will have succeeded and this prison planet will be nothing but a bad memory."

"And I will be cashiered, out of a job, will have lost my pension—the works."

"And many a human being will be alive and happy who would have been miserable or dead. Besides, the military is no place for a grown man. And with a million credits in the bank you can buy lawyers, live the good life, forget your past."

"What million?"

"The bribe that I am going to pay into a numbered account for you to make all of this worth your while."

He shook his fist. "You are a crook, diGriz! Do you think that I would stoop to your criminal, crooked level?"

"No. But you might be the administrator of the Save Liokukae Fund which has been set up by an anonymous benefactor."

He scowled, opened his mouth to protest. Stopped. Burst out laughing.

"Jim—you are something else again! What the hell—I'll do it. But on *my* terms, understand?"

"Understood. Just tell me where to mail the check."

"All right. Now let's get you a uniform while I forge some shipping orders. I have the feeling that I am going to enjoy being a civilian."

"You will, you will. Shall we go?"

We went. Marching in step in a most military manner. Marching into the future, into a better, brighter future.

The blues had been sung. A page turned, a chapter ended. Tremearne would do a good job of sorting out this repellent world. I would do equally well as I slipped away between the interstices of society.

In six months I would be far from here, my trail cold, my bank account filled, my life more interesting. Once rested and restored—it would indeed be time for The Stainless Steel Rat to ride again!

## AND YOU WILL SING THE BLUES TOO . . .

. . . if you don't speak Esperanto. A number of readers, from a number of countries, have written to me asking if there is such a language as Esperanto. There is! Jim diGriz speaks it like a native—as do most of the people he meets while involved in his interstellar trade. Esperanto is doing fine in the future—but does it exist in the present?

It certainly does. It is a growing, living, simple second language for millions of speakers around the world. It is easy to learn—and fun to use. There are many books, magazines and even newspapers published in Esperanto.

If you are interested in more information, The Stainless Steel Rat's advice—and mine as well—is to call this number:

(800) 828-5944

or send a postcard with your name and address to:

ESPERANTO
P.O. Box 1129
El Cerrito, CA 94530

It will change your life!

Harry Harrison